# THREE MONTHS TO FOREVER

HUDSON LIN

YELLOW LANTERN PRESS

# CONTENTS

Three Months to Forever

© 2020 Hudson Lin.

First edition published in 2018 by Dreamspinner Press.

Cover Art

© 2020 Zoe York

Cover content is for illustrative purposes only and any person depicted on the cover is a model.

Formatting

© 2020 Allison Temple



eBook ISBN: 978-1-9993812-3-3

Paperback ISBN: 978-1-9993812-4-0

v. 2.0

❀ Created with Vellum

Three Months to Forever

By Hudson Lin

Ben is looking for an adventure when he accepts a temporary assignment in Hong Kong, but he never anticipates how his life might change when he meets a sophisticated, intriguing man named Sai. Their initial attraction is sizzling and soon grows into more as Sai takes Ben on a tour of the city's famous landmarks and introduces him to the local cuisine. Sai stimulates Ben's intellect and curiosity, and for jaded corporate lawyer Sai, Ben's innocent eagerness is a breath of fresh air. It would be so easy to fall in love....

But nothing is that simple. Sai's job forces him to do things that violate his morals, and the difficult dynamics with his family is a major obstacle to any lasting relationship with Ben. For Ben, he misses his family back in Toronto, and can he really leave behind his home for a man he's only known a short time? With the clock ticking, they must decide whether to risk it all and turn three months into forever.

**1**

———

riday, September 1

"AND TO those who are new in town, welcome to Hong Kong! Your first drink is on the house!"

Ben Dutton leaned against the bar as the host with the heavy French accent stepped off the mini stage. The rooftop patio overlooked the city of Hong Kong, and all around him were people of varying ethnicities and accents, still dressed in business suits for the after-work networking event, sipping free alcohol and passing out business cards.

He stifled a yawn right as a bartender placed the beer he ordered in front of him on the bar.

"Thanks," Ben mumbled. He was surprised he was still awake. Having just arrived in Hong Kong from Toronto the day before, jet lag was quickly setting in, and the only thing keeping him going was sheer determination.

Ben searched for the coworker he'd arrived with, but there was no sign of Mo on the dimly lit patio. Instead his gaze landed upon two men chatting animatedly down the bar from him. One was tall and slim, hair artfully spiked, sipping delicately from a martini glass. The other was shorter, with a plain but neat haircut, strong eyebrows, and a sharply tailored suit.

Ben's gaydar pinged, but in his current stage of fatigue, it was more like a dull buzz. They'd make a cute couple, his half-asleep brain thought. The taller one threw his head back and laughed out loud while the shorter one glowered at his companion.

Ben blinked and then blinked again, much more slowly. His eyes shot open when his head started lolling forward, and the sight that greeted Ben was the shorter man staring at him with a crease between his brows.

Shit, he'd been caught falling asleep. He tried a hesitant smile and a nod but got no reaction. Then the taller man turned with a questioning expression that melted into a smile—with a wave of a martini glass and a tilt of his head, Ben guessed he'd been invited over.

"Hi, sorry," Ben apologized, his default when at a loss for words.

"Why do you apologize?" The taller man spoke first with clearly articulated English, if heavy with a Chinese accent. "Don't be sorry. We like it when handsome men notice us."

A blush heated Ben's ears at the sly compliment. "Uh, thanks?"

The taller man smiled and held out his hand. "I'm Winston Chiu."

"Oh. Ben Dutton."

"And this is Kwok Sai Hei." Winston introduced his friend, but the Chinese name was said so fast and sounded so foreign to Ben's Canadian ears that he was too embarrassed to admit he hadn't caught it.

The shorter man took pity on him with a small, knowing grin. "Just call me Sai."

"Sai, okay. Sai, yeah, that's a lot easier. Sorry, all these Chinese names are kind of hard to keep straight. Or wait, is it Cantonese? Or is Cantonese the same thing as Chinese? Oh God. I must sound like such an idiot. Sorry. I'm sorry. I'm really jet-lagged right now. That's not an excuse or anything, just... I'm sorry."

Ben rubbed his eyes. If only he could hit the rewind button on the past few minutes. When he dared to glance up again, Winston was barely holding in his laughter, but Sai didn't look nearly as amused.

"It's okay," Winston said. "Did you arrive in Hong Kong recently?"

"Yeah." Ben ran a hand over his face, noting the stubble scraping against his palm. "Yesterday. From Canada."

Winston's brows shot up. "You arrived yesterday, and you're already hard at work networking."

Ben chuckled and shook his head. "Not so much networking as making a fool of myself, apparently." He snuck a glance at Sai, who gazed out at the mingling groups of people as if he wanted to bail on this conversation.

"So, Ben, how long are you in town for?" Winston asked.

"Three months." Ben launched into the spiel he'd been giving to people since he first got approved for the temporary assignment. "I work for BMO Private Bank. We've been growing our client base in Asia quite rapidly over the past couple of years. They've decided to create a client onboarding team in region to provide more timely support, so they've pulled some staff from Canada to help get the team up and running."

Winston nodded with a polite, if uninterested smile. "I don't know anything about banking." He shrugged, then sipped his martini.

"Right." Ben chuckled. "Sorry." And he took a sip of his beer.

"What part of Canada are you from? Vancouver?"

The abrupt question from Sai took Ben a little by surprise, and it was a moment before he pulled his answer together. "Oh, um, no, I'm from Toronto."

Sai nodded and turned back to gazing across the room, leaving Ben feeling like he had given the wrong answer. "But I've been to Vancouver before. It's a beautiful city," he said, trying to make up for it.

Sai gave another disinterested nod, and Ben smiled through the awkwardness.

If it was awkward for Winston, though, he didn't show it. "Three months is not very much time to explore Hong Kong," he noted.

"I know." Ben chuckled. "I've been making a mental list of everything I want to see."

"Sai could show you around." Winston grinned at his friend and got back a skeptical glare.

"Really? That'd be so great. I'd love to see the city with someone who's local and knows all the hidden gems. Oh, but of course I wouldn't want to impose or anything. I mean, you probably have better things to do than show a random stranger around town, right?" Ben forced out a laugh and chased it with a long swig of his beer.

He really should leave and find his bed. The jet lag was making him dumb. Yes, that was it. It had nothing to do with the way Sai pinned him with an intense look, dark-brown eyes almost black in the dim lighting, lips pressed firmly together in a way that made Ben's breath hitch.

"Oh, Ben, you're very cute, you know." Winston laughed.

Ben laughed along, except he wasn't sure the joke wasn't on him. Sai continued to stare, and Ben didn't quite know what to do with himself under such protracted scrutiny. Only when Sai looked away, turning his gaze back out to the party behind them, could Ben breathe freely again.

"So, uh, how did you guys get connected to this event?" Ben asked, focusing on Winston, who felt like the safer option. "I thought this was primarily for expats."

Winston nodded. "It is. But the host is my boyfriend." He flicked his eyes to the French guy who had given the opening remarks at the beginning of the night. "Jacques!" he shouted above the din and waved his hand in the air.

It only took a minute for Jacques to join them. "Hello, gentlemen. I hope you are having a good evening." He held out a hand to Ben. "I'm Jacques Renard. Are you new here? I do not think we've met before."

"Yes, he's new here," Winston jumped in as Ben shook Jacques's hand. "From Canada, here for three months, works in banking."

Jacques nodded as if that was all he needed to know about Ben's background. "Fantastic. Welcome to Hong Kong." Then to Winston, "Darling, may I steal you away from your friends?"

Winston gave them a smile, not apologetic at all, and went off whispering in Jacques's ear. An uncomfortable silence settled between Ben and Sai, and he scrambled for something to say.

"So do you know the best places to party?"

Mortification painted his ears red as his words registered in his brain. Best places to party? He sounded like some kid with a newly acquired taste for freedom. Ben knew he looked young for his twenty-nine years, no thanks to the baby fat he never really grew out of. But that was the last impression he wanted to give Sai.

Sai, with the faint lines across his forehead and the grays peppering his hair, exuded an air of command that did strange things to Ben's body. Sai gave him a once-over with casual authority, his gaze like a heated laser, traveling over Ben's face, down his neck, and then sweeping across his body. He burned under Sai's examination, a fire that came from within and competed with the stifling heat of Hong Kong in September.

"Yes," Sai said, and Ben almost forgot what his original question was. Sai looked away, a slight crease in his brow. "Many of the gay bars are in the Sheung Wan area. Not too far from here. Do you know where that is?"

That was the longest string of words Sai had spoken to him all evening. And Sai's voice was a fascinating mix of accents, mostly North American, just a hint of Chinese, much lighter than Winston's, and a noticeable dash of British. It added to that dark allure that had Ben's mouth growing dry.

Ben tugged at the tie already hanging loose around his neck and undid an extra button on his shirt. The way Sai watched his every move was not helping Ben's state of over-heating or his ability to think.

"Um...." Ben blinked. He could have sworn Sai had asked him a question. Oh, right, Sheung Wan. "Yes, I know that area. In fact, that's where I'm staying."

Sai nodded. "In a serviced apartment?"

"Yes, exactly. It's really nice. Everything's furnished, and there's daily housekeeping. They even provide laundry service if I don't feel like doing it myself. I mean, I usually do my own laundry at home. It's not like I don't know how to do laundry. It's just now there's a choice." Ben trailed off in an awkward laugh and sipped his beer to fill the silence. "Um, your English is very good." It was the first thing that popped into his head.

Sai frowned and pressed his lips firmly into a thin line. Oh God, what a stupid thing to say. This guy spent time around foreigners; of course his English was good.

"Thank you," Sai deadpanned. "I'm glad it passes muster for a native speaker."

Shit, Sai was offended. But there was a slight twitch of his lips, and the corners of his eyes crinkled. So maybe not offended? Oh God, Ben didn't know. None of the social signs were the same here, and he couldn't read the intention behind the words like he could back home.

"Did you study abroad?" He managed not to cringe at his own question.

Except this time Sai gave a short chuckle and broke out in a reserved smile. "Yes, I studied at Cornell for undergraduate studies and then Columbia for law school. Before that I did my schooling at an international school here."

"Oh." At least his guess hadn't been completely off base. "So you're a lawyer? What kind of law?"

"Corporate."

"Oh, that's cool." Ben took a long swig of his beer, conscious of the way Sai's eyes lingered on his throat. He was so distracted that he forgot to swallow and then sputtered when the alcohol overflowed in his mouth. He coughed while wiping his mouth with the back of his hand. Sai dropped his gaze to the floor, thank God, though he looked like he could barely contain his laughter.

"Are you okay?" Sai asked after Ben finally got his windpipe working again.

"Yeah." He cleared his throat. "Sorry about that."

Sai shook his head, dismissing the apology. "Wouldn't want you choking on your beer on your second day in Hong Kong. What kind of first impression would that be for us?"

"Oh, no, there's no danger of that, believe me. This city is really cool. I mean, I haven't seen much of it yet. But what I have seen, I really love." Ben couldn't read what Sai's grin meant, or why Sai's dark eyes looked like they were laughing at him. But there was no ignoring the fluttering in his stomach that only grew with each passing moment in Sai's presence.

Sai narrowed his eyes and tilted his head up to meet Ben's taller height. The slight movement was the only indication to Ben he had been swaying unconsciously toward Sai. He caught himself but couldn't quite move back; it was as if he'd been caught by some invisible net Sai had cast, held in place solely by the look in Sai's eyes.

"Ben!"

Sai flicked his gaze away at the sound of his name, and the net was let loose. Ben stepped back and took a couple of breaths to steady his racing heart before looking for the source of the voice. Mo waved him over to talk to a group of people who looked a lot less interesting than Sai.

"Uh, that's my friend, Mo. He also works at BMO. He's from Vancouver." That was probably too much irrelevant information, but Ben was so far down the embarrassment hole by that point it didn't make much of a difference.

Sai nodded with that slight crinkle around the edge of his eyes and the little upturn of his lips.

"I, uh, should probably go see what he wants." Which was the last thing Ben wanted to do, so he made no move to leave.

"Ben!" Mo shouted again. "I want to introduce you to some people!"

Still Ben hesitated, hoping Sai would offer up something to continue their conversation, to maintain this strange connection, whatever it was. As curious as the feeling in his gut was, Ben liked it and wanted more of it.

But Sai didn't give him an out. Instead he smiled, polite and formal. "It was nice meeting you, Ben Dutton."

"Yeah, you too. I'll, uh, just say hi to them and be right back." Maybe he was too desperate, but so be it.

Sai gave him a short nod that held no promises, and Ben relented to Mo's summons. He went and introduced himself to the random people Mo wanted him to meet, made some small talk, and then turned back to the spot where he and Sai had had their moment. He didn't know what he expected: maybe Sai still standing there, waiting for him with those smoldering dark eyes and teasing grin? But there was no sign of him.

Ben sighed. Well, shit.


Monday, September 4


BEN FOLLOWED Macey, the local compliance officer, into the meeting room for his compliance orientation.

"I heard Mo's already dragged you out to some parties," she said as they sat at the round table.

"Yeah, a networking event on Friday. And then I spent most of the weekend sleeping, to be honest." Making a fool of himself with those two local guys had been more than enough motivation for him to get over his jet lag.

"Did he tell you about Happy Valley on Wednesday?" Macey pulled some papers out of a clear plastic folder.

"That's the horse racing, right?"

Macey nodded.

"And then there's some boat trip next weekend?" Trying to keep all the social events straight was as difficult as adjusting to the new work environment. Ben had an active personal life back in Toronto, but nothing quite like horse racing and hanging out on a yacht all in one week.

"That's Hong Kong for you: work hard, play hard. We take both very seriously." She spoke with such a solemn expression that Ben wasn't sure if she was joking. "Honestly, though, it's good to have you guys here. Stella's been complaining for ages about how frustrating it is to send information back and forth to Canada with the time difference. BMO's really moving up the ranks in Asia in the private banking sector, business is exploding, and we need people on the ground here."

She handed him a couple of stapled packets. "Here you go. This is the Hong Kong compliance manual, which is basically an addendum to the global manual. The bulk of it deals with local requirements for the Hong Kong Securities and Futures Commission. However, since you will not be advising on securities, you do not need to be registered with the SFC."

Ben nodded his understanding. The fact that on-boarding staff didn't need to register with the local financial regulatory authority was one of the main reasons why Ben and other Canadians had been able to go to Hong Kong on short notice. They were responsible for setting up new client accounts and wire transfer instructions, running anti-money-laundering checks to make sure the bank wasn't complicit in illegal money movements, and making sure client files were complete under regulatory requirements. The relationship managers brought in new clients, the portfolio analysts gave investment advice; Ben's team made sure all the logistics ran smoothly in the background. Some said it was a boring job. Sometimes Ben thought it was too, but he was good at it—one of the best performers on his team, in fact.

Macey spent the next twenty minutes going over the rest of the compliance manual and the local employee hand-book. None of it was surprising to Ben; all the workplace safety policies were similar to those in Canada.

As they were wrapping up, Macey asked, "Have you been to Hong Kong before?"

"No, it's my first time in Asia." Ben gathered his things and stood.

"What made you want to come now?" Macey flicked off

the light switch and shut the meeting room door behind them.

Ben had been asked that question a lot in the few short weeks between when his assignment had been approved and when he had to jump on a plane to the other side of the planet. If he was honest, though, he wasn't entirely sure why he had put his hand up when management asked for volunteers to go to Hong Kong. It had almost been a whim, something he did on impulse just to see what would happen.

He knew next to nothing about Hong Kong and didn't speak the language; he never thought they'd pick him of all people. But he knew how to do the job and he was available to leave for an extended period of time on very short notice. Whatever the reason, Ben was glad for the opportunity. It might have started out as a whim, but deep in the marrow of his bones, he knew it was the right thing to do—it was something he had to do, like something was waiting for him on the other side of the world.

"I've always wanted to see this part of the world," he said. Macey didn't need a lengthy confession of his philosophical yearnings.

"I grew up in Toronto," Macey said. "But my family is from Hong Kong. Moving back here was probably the best decision I've ever made. You'll love it."

Ben hoped so.

**2**

---

$\mathcal{W}$ednesday, September 6

THE THUNDEROUS roar of hooves against the sandy ground echoed past, drowning out the shouts of the crowd gathered at the Happy Valley Racecourse. Ben added his voice to the din and pumped his hand in the air, only to have his beer spill all over his arm.

"Ah fuck!" He laughed, shaking off the excess alcohol.

"Ha, bro! You suck at this," Mo shouted at him with a giant smile on his face. "You keep betting on the slow-ass horses!"

"Fuck off," Ben threw back as he tried to brush away the alcohol before it soaked into the rolled-up sleeve of his dress shirt. "Shit. I've got to go find napkins."

He headed toward the food stands, weaving between groups of spectators chatting loudly about which horse to bet on for the next race. He ducked past lines of people waiting to take photos with some costumed cartoon character he didn't recognize and finally spotted a napkin dispenser next to a condiments table.

"Ben Dutton?"

Ben glanced up at his name and didn't recognize any of the faces around him until he did a double-take and landed on one staring intently back at him. Dark eyes, firmly pressed lips, and neatly cut black hair. Sai. Oh God. Sai.

"Hey!" He could hear the slightly over-the-top enthusiasm in his voice and decided to try again with a little more moderation. "Hey, Sai. How's it going?"

"I'm doing well. Are you okay?" Sai nodded to Ben's handful of napkins.

"What? Oh yeah. I'm good. I just spilled beer all over myself."

"I see." Amusement tinged Sai's eyes and made Ben's stomach flutter in anticipation. He forgot where he was for a moment, lost in the hold Sai had over him. Then Sai cocked his head, and the spell was broken.

Ben tossed the soiled napkins in the nearby garbage bin and shifted from one foot to the other, unsure where to look and what to say.

"Are you here with your colleagues?" Sai's intonation dipped in unexpected places; it was a siren song to Ben's ears.

"Yeah. They're, uh, over by the rails over there." He waved his hand toward the end of the track.

Sai nodded before speaking. "Do you remember Winston?"

Winston, right, Sai's friend. "Yeah, yeah, of course I remember him. He's with the French guy, right?"

Sai chuckled. "Jacques, yes. We've got a box up there." He looked over his shoulder at a blocked-off area of the bleachers, and Ben spotted Winston watching them with blatant interest. "Would you care to join us?"

Ben thought for a split second about Mo and the rest of his coworkers and then dismissed them. "Yeah, sure. I'd love to."

"What about your colleagues?" Sai looked skeptical.

Ben shrugged. "I'll just message them. It's fine."

Sai gave a short nod and turned on his heel, not waiting to see if Ben followed. From his perch above, Winston tracked their progress. Sai didn't look back even once. By the time they got to the reserved box, Ben wondered if Sai actually wanted to invite him or if Winston forced his hand.

"Ben!" Winston greeted him as if they were old friends.

"Hi, Winston. It's good to see you again," Ben replied. Sai took up a spot next to the railing several steps away.

"I should not be surprised to see you here. Was Happy Valley on your list of things to see while in Hong Kong?" Winston asked.

"Yeah, it was. Everyone keeps talking about it all the time, so I wanted to check it out."

"Is there something similar in Toronto?"

Ben stole a quick glance at Sai before answering. "There's a racecourse, but horse racing isn't as popular in Toronto as it is here."

"I see." Winston flicked his eyes to Sai and back and then curled his lips in a grin.

Was his interest in Sai that obvious? Ben ducked his head as his ears burned red.

"Well, it was good to see you, Ben. I'm sure Sai could use some company."

Winston might as well have winked at him, for all his words implied. But when Ben was left alone to approach Sai, he hesitated.

Sai was leaning over, forearms resting on the railing, hands cradling his plastic cup of beer, his back an elegant line that ended in a pert ass covered in suit slacks. He watched the giant screen that showed a live feed of the horses set to run the next race, along with statistics Ben had given up trying to understand.

A shroud of mystery blanketed Sai, and it aroused Ben's curiosity more than anything ever had in a long time. Perhaps it was because Sai was older and exuded a quiet confidence that came with experience.

A thrill of nervous anticipation ran up Ben's spine as he approached and mimicked Sai's posture against the railing. Sai spared him a single glance, a subtle sigh, and a slight smile, then turned his attention back to the screen.

"So I've been reading up about the history of Hong Kong." In fact, Ben had spent all of Sunday night researching. "It's interesting how China lost the city to the British during the opium wars, then ninety-nine years under British rule, then reverting back to China in 1997. I have some friends back home whose families moved to Canada because of that. They said they wanted to leave because of the whole communism thing. And the protests a couple of years ago? It all sounds pretty tumultuous."

Sai stared at him, and the silence stretched for a couple of seconds past comfortable. Ben's ears burned hot before Sai spoke. "You've been doing your homework."

Ben ducked his head and gave a one-shoulder shrug. "I guess."

Sai chuckled. "I'm impressed. That's probably more than most other foreigners know about Hong Kong."

"Really?" Ben turned to face Sai, leaning his hip against the rail. "That's surprising. If they're living here, why wouldn't they want to know the history of the place?"

Sai narrowed his eyes at him, pausing almost as if he didn't believe Ben was sincere. "I suppose that since Hong Kong isn't their home, they don't feel a need to know."

"Oh. That's too bad. I feel like there's a really rich history here." And he meant it. He really did. His journey down the rabbit hole of the internet had led him through a series of websites about Hong Kong culture and the Cantonese language. He'd learned locals referred to most foreigners somewhat flippantly as gweilo, or "foreign devil," and there was such a thing as Hong Kong-style diner cuisine, courtesy of decades as a British colony.

Sai straightened, placing them much closer to each other than would be typical for practical strangers making small talk. And the look in his eyes kicked up the fluttering in Ben's stomach to a whole other level. The air suddenly felt a little too thin.

"Why are you so interested?" Sai asked.

"I don't know." Ben dropped his gaze away from Sai's intent stare. "I'm here for three months. I guess I just want to know the place."

"You could just as easily go to parties every night and all weekend long. Have a good time and then go home."

It felt like a test to Ben, like his response would determine the path of their future acquaintance. "If I wanted to party, I could have stayed home. I came here because...." He swallowed around his suddenly dry mouth. "Because I want to be here."

Ben snuck his tongue out to wet his lips, and Sai dropped his gaze to follow the movement. The fluttering in his stomach seemed to settle into a peaceful calm the longer he spent in Sai's presence, and Ben hoped to God he had passed the test. He swayed a little closer and could have sworn Sai leaned in too. The moment's momentum was sweeping them toward what Ben was sure would be a scorching-hot kiss. Sai stiffened at the last second, smiled politely, and backed away.

Oxygen rushed back into his lungs, but Ben couldn't help the keen sense of disappointment. He wanted to know how Sai's lips would feel under his own. Would they be hard and demanding? Or soft and pliant? They'd probably be both. One could dream.

Sai turned back to the giant screen showing the horses already in their starting blocks. A buzzer sounded, the gates blew open, and off they went, kicking up sand, eating up distance, and rounding the track with their colorfully attired jockeys leaning gracefully into the turn.

As the horses ran, Ben's attention was on Sai next to him. The way he tucked in his chin and assumed a posture of casual authority. The way he slipped his hands into his pockets, shoulders held down and back, nonchalant yet powerful. Ben shifted on his feet to hide the shudder running up his spine.

The horses raced across the finish line to the uproar of the spectators, but Ben was deaf to all of it. "So how would you recommend I go about learning more about Hong Kong?"

Sai turned his dark eyes to him, and Ben sucked in a breath at the heat in them; there was no mistaking the raw desire Sai cast his way.

"We're going to a local bar after the last race," Sai said.

Was it Ben's imagination, or was Sai's voice a couple notes lower than before?

"Would you like to join us?"

A sharp spike of excitement rushed through him, but Ben couched his expression and simply nodded and pretended to consider the offer. "Sure."

Sai's lips curled in slow motion, ending in a knowing smile.

They ended up at LINQ, a nondescript bar Ben had walked past before without realizing what it was. Wednesday night was apparently Guys' Night, and the doors were thrown wide open, with customers spilling out onto the street. Inside, the small space was crammed with men, all of them laughing, drinking, touching arms and shoulders and waists.

There was a table reserved for them near the back, and a waiter appeared as they took their seats. Local and imported beer and well-made gin and tonics flowed freely for the rest of the night, and the more they all drank, the more intense the conversation got.

Ben found himself asking controversial questions about Hong Kong politics, and Sai, Winston, and some other friend, whom Ben had not formally met, yelled their arguments across the table.

Gone was the quiet, reserved Sai from earlier. Instead, Sai leaned his elbow against the table and gestured with his hands while he spoke, slapping the tabletop with the flats of his fingers when making a particularly heated point or when one of his friends put up a statement he disagreed with. When not speaking, he often settled his free hand on Ben's shoulder, its weight comforting and secure in a way Ben had never experienced before.

They discussed the student protestors who took to the streets every couple of years in opposition of Beijing's influence in local politics. And how the unrest was fueled by the lack of opportunities and well-paying jobs for Hong Kong's youth. They argued over whether the local economy favored the super-rich and left large chunks of the population living well below the poverty line. Ben couldn't follow all of it, but what he understood was fascinating.

More intriguing, though, was the way Sai spoke with passion and fervor about each topic, presenting facts and statistics crafted in articulate arguments Ben was in no position to dispute. He might have been biased, but Ben felt pretty sure none of Sai's friends could dispute them either.

When the discussion died down, Ben settled back in his

seat and leaned over to Sai. "You seem really passionate about social justice issues."

Sai appeared surprised at Ben's observation. "I suppose you could say that."

"You said you work in corporate law?"

"Yes, that's right."

"Sounds like you should be in human rights law instead."

Sai stilled, and Ben wondered if he'd said something wrong. Sai's dark eyes looked even darker in the dim lighting of the bar, and intense as if he was trying to suss out something about Ben. Ben had nothing to hide, but Sai's examination was protracted and thorough. He ducked his head, and Sai barked out a short laugh, reaching for his gin and tonic. Ben followed with a quiet chuckle.

"Oh, Ben." Sai dropped his empty glass back on the table, his tone laced heavily with sarcasm. "Human rights are for those with hearts that bleed. It is not for those who understand how the world works and seek to be on top."

Ben drew his brows together. Was he supposed to have recognized the saying? It sounded cold and extreme.

"That is what my father said when I told him I wanted to pursue human rights law." Sai set his glass on the table with a bang. "He decided I should pursue corporate law instead."

"Wait, he decided for you?" Ben wasn't quite sure he understood that correctly.

Sai's smile took on a hint of sadness. "You wanted to learn more about Hong Kong and its people." He waved his hand. "Welcome to Hong Kong."

A heavy hand landed on Ben's shoulder, and he looked up, startled, to find Winston standing over them. "Whatever he's telling you, do not believe him." Winston spoke in words a little too slurred to take seriously. "Things are never as bad as Sai thinks they are. Come on." He tugged at both of their arms. "We're getting the DJ to play our music. It's time to dance!"

Sai tried to wave them off, but Ben liked the idea of dancing, and he especially liked the idea of dancing with Sai. They dragged Sai out of his seat and pushed their table closer to the wall to create a makeshift dance floor.

Sai wasn't much of a dancer, but that was fine by Ben. He could dance enough for the both of them. He worked the small space to his advantage, brushing his arm, his back, and his hip against Sai. A blaze of heat ripped through him when Sai latched his hand on to his hip and held him in place as they swayed together.

At some point Ben's arms found their way around Sai's neck, and Sai pulled them closer until they bumped chests. Ben was taller than Sai by a couple of inches, had a bigger frame, and certainly weighed more. But Ben felt deliciously small when he looked into Sai's eyes and saw something strong and in control. He trembled under the intensity of Sai's gaze, and he loved the feeling.

Last call was announced over the music, and the interruption sent a spike of panic through Ben, jolting him out of his happy, lusty daze. He wasn't ready to let Sai go, but Sai was already pulling away.

Ben pulled him back and said the first thing that came to mind: "My friends and I are going on a junk boat this Saturday. Come with us."

Sai speared him with a look that said he was crazy. Maybe he was crazy, crazy to think this intelligent, knowledgeable, and sophisticated man would want to spend any time with a nobody like him. But he had to try. He held his breath and waited for the answer.

It came a couple of moments late. But then Sai's look softened, and his lips curled in an amused grin. "Okay. I'll come."

## 3

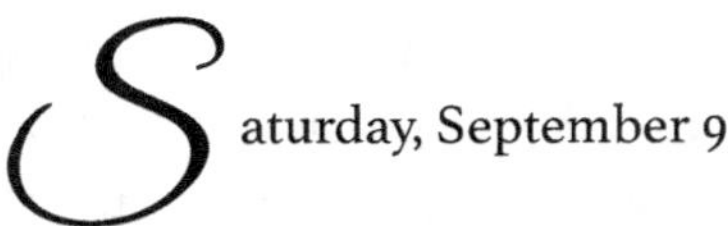

**S**aturday, September 9

WHAT THE hell was he thinking? Sai stood on the dock, staring at the junk boat and wondering if he should just bail. He must have been much too drunk that night at the bar with Ben asking all those questions about Hong Kong.

Sai remembered his heated diatribes as Ben had looked on with those adoring blue eyes and blond lashes. They were just a shade darker than the shockingly light hair on his head, had been damp with the sweat of Hong Kong's tropical climate and the number of bodies squeezed into the small bar. And how could he forget the feel of Ben's body as they'd held each other, solid and soft at the same time, more than enough man to fill Sai's arms?

When Ben whispered the invitation in his ear, he had been powerless to refuse. So there he was on a Saturday morning, staring at a junk boat that was really a yacht marketed to tourists as a traditional fishing boat. There was nothing traditional about it—gleaming white, with a brilliant-blue awning above the top deck. Sai would bet a year's salary they had one of those giant inflatable slides on board so thrill-seekers could launch themselves off the top and into the water.

"Sai!" Ben's excited voice rang out, and Sai spotted him standing on the deck of the boat, waving his hand high in the air. Too late to bail now.

He squared his shoulders and soldiered forward. Handing his bag off to one of the crew members, he ignored their outstretched hand and hoisted himself up onto the deck with an ease that came from years of boarding yachts belonging to his father's friends.

Ben lumbered over, a little unsteady as an unexpected wave pushed the boat against the dock. Instead of a customary wave or handshake by way of greeting, he pulled Sai in for a full-body hug. Sai stiffened at the sudden familiarity of the touch and then relaxed into the embrace as his body responded to holding Ben in his arms.

"You made it!"

He couldn't help but smile at Ben's enthusiasm. It was a little over the top, he had to admit, but it seemed genuine enough, and something about that was refreshing in a simple, effortless way.

"Let me introduce you to everyone." Ben dragged him over to a group of expats already in states of semidress, with only their swimming attire on. "This is Mo. That's Stella, Macey, and Heather. They're all from BMO. Mo and Heather are on assignment like me. Stella and Macey are here permanently. Guys, this is Sai."

He nodded to each one in turn as Ben introduced them. They were a mixed crowd of varying ethnicities, pretty typical in expat circles, but Sai was probably the only native Hong Kong person, and that left him with the strange feeling of being the outsider in his own city.

"Hey! You're friends with Jacques and Winston?" Mo came up and offered his hand.

"Yes, that's right," Sai replied.

"Cool, cool. They're an awesome couple." Mo clapped Sai on the shoulder. "Glad you could join us today. If you'll excuse me, I'm on sunscreen duty." He winked and headed back to the ladies, waving a bottle of sun cream in the air.

Mo's easy acceptance that they were gay was why Sai and Winston and their group of friends tended to gravitate toward foreigners: fewer snide looks and whispering behind hands, fewer subtly spoken words of disapproval or outright cold shoulders. Winston didn't give a shit about being out and proud, and he liked to rub it in the faces of their parents' friends that he was dating a man, a French man. But Sai was more reserved; he didn't feel the need to give the gossips any more fodder than they already had.

"Hey, Sai. You good?" Ben settled his hand on Sai's shoulder, and the heat of it seeped through Sai's shirt. Ben had a streak of white across his cheek, and with his wide grin and blue eyes sparkling in the sun, he looked adorable.

Ben must have read the intent in Sai's eyes because he licked his lips, and with one blink of those dark-blond lashes, his eyes filled with the same heat Sai felt.

"I'm doing very well."

Ben's breath hitched and satisfaction filled Sai in a way he hadn't expected it would.

"Hello, everybody!" one of the crew members called out for attention.

Sai reluctantly broke eye contact but stood close enough behind Ben to feel the heat radiating off his skin. The crew member gave out safety instructions, but Sai wasn't listening. His attention was on the rapid rise and fall of Ben's chest and the way he tried to conceal the shudder that ran through him when Sai's breath caressed his shoulder. There was something about Ben's wide blue eyes, pale-white skin, and good-natured demeanor that stirred Sai's desires in a way few of his previous partners had been able to.

The boat pulled away from the dock and motored out of Victoria Harbour for the two-and-a-half-hour trip to Tai Long Wan, considered by some to be one of the most beautiful beaches in all of Hong Kong. Their little group claimed a part of the top deck, and Sai settled in the shade while Ben stripped off his tank top and lay out in the sun.

From behind his sunglasses, Sai allowed himself the luxury of gazing upon Ben—he was solidly built, by no means muscle-bound, but rather slightly on the chubby side. His swimming shorts hung low across his hips, low enough to reveal two little dimples on his lower back, and Sai had to drag his gaze away as his imagination ran wild with images of pressing his thumbs into those dimples while he fucked Ben into the mattress.

It was going to be next to impossible to resist Ben with all that skin exposed and him casting sweet little smiles in Sai's direction. Sai closed his eyes. Damn Winston and his stupid meddling. The last thing he needed was his nosy friend pushing him toward easy hookups that were anything but easy. As if summoned by mere thoughts of him, Sai's phone pinged with an incoming message from Winston.

Winston: How is the boat trip? Did you fuck him yet?

Sai: Fuck you.

Winston: No, not me. Him.

Sai: Dick face.

Winston: You should have just fucked him after the club like I told you to.

Winston had a point. There had been a couple of openings during that night when Sai could have taken Ben home, slept with him, and moved on. But he had hesitated because, God damn, because Ben didn't feel like a one-night stand. Ben with his earnest questions and rapt attention deserved more than the "fuck 'em and leave 'em" Winston advocated.

Sai's gaze drifted back to Ben, who had turned over onto his back. A glossy sheen of sweat shone across his skin, and his hair, also wet with sweat, was a shade darker than normal.

Against his better judgment, Sai snagged the bottle of sun cream off the deck before sitting down in the narrow space beside Ben on his chaise lounge.

He gently shook Ben's shoulder, noting the heat of the skin under his hand. "Hey."

The sleepy deep inhale and the slow spread of a smile across Ben's lips did nothing to help cool Sai's arousal. And the quietly muttered hey and lazy stretch of arms made Sai want to flip Ben over and take him right there on the deck, surrounded by people.

"You're getting too much sun. Here." Sai ignored the way his voice lowered with lust. He handed Ben the sun cream and pressed his lips together when Ben closed his hand around Sai's own but didn't take the proffered bottle.

"Can you put it on me?"

Sai couldn't see Ben's eyes behind the sunglasses, but he didn't need to. The softly spoken words and the shallow rapid breaths between parted lips were all the encouragement he needed. He cast his gaze around the top deck; aside from their group, all of whom appeared passed out in the sun, there were only a couple of other passengers, all foreigners, minding their own business on the other side of the deck. Sai popped the lid open and squeezed out a generous dollop of the thick white cream.

The first contact of his palms against Ben's chest felt like touching fire. It was warm and alluring but dangerous if Sai let himself get too close. His body responded to the instant lustful attraction, helped along by Ben's little sigh of contentment.

Sai worked his way down Ben's chest and across his stomach. It was soft under his touch at first, but then his fingers wandered over to the side, and Ben tensed, revealing the hard muscles underneath.

"Ticklish?" Sai asked, his voice husky.

"Yes, very," Ben gasped.

Sai continued. Feeling emboldened by the slight tenting of Ben's swimming shorts, Sai snuck a couple of fingers down under the waistband, just to ensure full coverage, he told himself.

He tapped Ben on the hip. "Turn over." He smiled to himself when it took Ben a few extra seconds to pull himself together enough to follow directions.

With another dollop of sun cream, Sai started at Ben's wide shoulders and immediately encountered stiff, tight muscles. He dug his thumbs into the backs of Ben's traps and smirked at the moaned yes he got in response.

"Shh," he admonished and the moan turned into a whimper. The quick application of sun cream rapidly became a massage session as Sai sought out all the knots in Ben's back, and there were many. When he made it down to Ben's lower back, he couldn't help but wrap his fingers around Ben's waist; his thumbs fit in those two tempting dimples as if they'd been carved just for him.

His brain conjured up images of Ben underneath him in bed, his hands wrapped around Ben's waist while Ben whimpered and moaned. It would be so easy to fall into a relationship with Ben, though his inner attorney mounted argument after argument for why it would be a foolish idea. Ben was only here temporarily. Sai had a demanding job. And yet none of those arguments seemed to matter when

Ben sat up and turned to him, sunglasses discarded and eyes heavy-lidded with desire.

Ben's arms didn't take as long and yet it felt longer with Ben following Sai's progress with his eyes. He rubbed the cream around each finger of Ben's hand and massaged his thumb into Ben's palm. Then he repeated the whole thing with Ben's other arm. By the time he was done, Sai had made up his mind. Tonight he'd take Ben to bed.

"Thanks." Ben's voice was husky.

Sai nodded and retreated to his spot in the shade, crossing his legs to hide his erection. The rest of the boat ride out to Tai Long Wan was comparatively uneventful, if Sai discounted how hyperaware he was of Ben's every movement and his every uttered word. When the crew dropped anchor away from the shore, he joined Ben by the railing looking out onto the pristine white-sand beach and the clear rich-blue water that turned aquamarine closer to land. The boat's engine shut off, and a peaceful quiet descended upon them.

"Oh my God, this is gorgeous." Ben looked a little dumbfounded, and Sai had to chuckle.

"It is. I haven't been here in years, and never by boat. It's easy to forget how beautiful Hong Kong is when we spend all our time in the city."

"I need to take a picture of this. My parents won't believe it." Ben scrambled for his phone and snapped a couple of shots of the beach before pulling Sai closer. "Come on, let's take a selfie."

Sai hesitated for a split second before giving in. He hated selfies and refused to participate when Winston insisted on them. But Ben tugged on his arm, flashed that silly grin, and Sai found himself giving in without a fight.

A loud splash disturbed the newfound quiet, and a roar ripped through the air as the crew began inflating a giant floating slide. It was triangular in shape, oversized steps on one side and a steep slope on the other.

"Oh my God, that's the slide!" Ben said with barely contained excitement.

Sai resisted the urge to bury his face in his hands. He had guessed it: there was the inflatable slide for all the thrill-seekers' pleasure.

"Ben! Are you seeing this?" Mo shouted over to them above the roar.

"Yeah, that's fucking huge!" Ben shouted back.

"That's what I'm talking about!"

Sai suddenly felt so old next to their youthful enthusiasm. Not that they were that young, he reminded himself. And he wasn't really that old. But the six- or seven-year gap that spanned their late twenties to his midthirties felt like generations.

Ben plucked Sai's T-shirt. "You're not wearing that in the water, are you?"

Sai wasn't sure if he even wanted to get into the water.

"You're definitely coming in the water. Don't even look at me like that." Ben turned and tossed his stuff in his bag.

Sai's protest died on his tongue.

"Come on!" Ben stood at the ladder leading to the lower deck. Everyone else had gone down already.

He shot Ben a skeptical look and got a silly grin in return. His resolve crumbled quickly at that grin. Okay, he'd go into the water. But there was no way in hell he was climbing up on that inflatable monstrosity.

Sai peeled off his T-shirt and stuck it in his bag, along with his sunglasses. When he turned back to Ben, he was openly ogling Sai's chest. Sai strode over to the ladder, enjoying how Ben tracked his movements.

"After you." He let his voice drop low.

Ben's breath hitched, and it was a few seconds before he moved to follow Sai's directions.

Despite the heat of the air, the water was cold. Cold enough that Sai wanted to climb back onto the boat. Cold enough to cool the raging libido he had been battling for the past two and a half hours. He stayed in the water.

"Whoa! This water is so warm!" Ben shouted as he floated a few feet away.

Crazy Canadians. Sai grabbed one of the pool noodles the crew had thrown overboard and paddled his way over to where Ben's group of friends gathered next to the slide.

"Who's going first?" Mo asked.

"We are!" one of the girls, Heather, maybe, shouted and swam toward the oversized steps, using the hand straps to pull herself up. The other girls followed her, and Mo was not far behind.

"Come on!" Ben nodded toward the slide, but Sai shook his head.

"You go ahead with your friends. I'll meet you on the other side." Sai waved him off and started for the other end of the slide to watch them all flail as they fell into the water, screaming.

"Fine!" Ben shouted as Sai swam away. "But you're coming next time!"

Sai waved at him and parked himself just out of range of the human projectiles hurdling down the thick wet nylon. When it was Ben's turn, he looked right at Sai, winked, and launched himself off the top. He landed in the water with a huge splash and mini tidal waves that had Sai shaking the salty seawater out of his eyes.

The smile on Ben's face could not have been any wider as he swam up, and Sai had to restrain himself from pulling him in for a sloppy, wet kiss.

"That was awesome!" Ben laughed. "You've got to try it."

"I don't think that's a good idea." Sai smiled back.

"Why not?"

"Yeah, why not?" Mo echoed from a few feet away.

"Come on, Sai!" Heather joined in, and so did the two other girls until he finally relented.

He narrowed his eyes at Ben and got a grin and a wink in return. Oh, Ben was going to pay for those winks later.

He followed Ben up the steps and found that it wasn't as difficult to climb up as he had thought. At least not as difficult when he had Ben's ass in his face, barely covered by the thin material of his swim shorts, wiggling back and forth as they climbed.

At the top they sat side by side, and Ben surprised him by reaching over and grabbing his hand. The warmth of Ben's grip, strong and sure, caused a swell of emotion to rise in Sai's chest, but he didn't have time to examine the feelings. Ben pushed off and dragged Sai with him into the water. Sai had just enough time to suck in a breath before he plunged under the clear blue, and he sputtered and laughed when he resurfaced.

Okay, they were right: that was fun. And the racing of his heart had nothing to do with the lingering warmth he felt from holding Ben's hand.

"Good?" Ben asked, water droplets hanging off his long lashes.

Sai let himself drift a little too close so their legs kicked and tangled together under the surface. The effect was immediate, and Sai was sure Ben's deep inhale wasn't due solely to the adrenaline from the slide.

"It was good," Sai conceded, his body responding to Ben's proximity. Thank God the water was cold.

Despite his earlier protest, Sai ended up enjoying the ugly, giant inflatable slide. By the time they were called back on board for lunch, Sai was exhausted. After lunch they took the little banana boat out to shore, and Ben's friends disappeared somewhere, leaving them to pick their way through the sunbathers spotting the beach.

"Thank you for inviting me today. It really is lovely out here." Sai stuck his hands into his pockets to keep himself from reaching for Ben.

"Oh, not a problem! I'm so glad you came." Ben paused. "I wasn't sure you would, you know."

"Why would you think that?"

"I don't know." He shrugged again. "You're so sophisticated. I didn't know if you'd want to spend an entire Saturday on a silly junk boat."

Ben's ears took on a distinct pink hue that was visible even through the tan he had accumulated that day. He looked down, focused on the sand, and Sai couldn't help but stare—he was beautiful.

"To be completely honest," Sai said, "I wasn't sure if I wanted to spend an entire Saturday on a junk boat either. But I'm glad I did come."

Sai stopped when Ben peeked up at him with the blue of his eyes showing through the blond lashes. It took every ounce of Sai's willpower not to take Ben by the shoulders and pull him in, to feel that body against his, to taste those lips with his own. For a couple of moments, it was touch and go, but Sai restrained himself and shuffled back a few inches, giving them both a little room to breathe.

He cleared his throat before continuing their walk. "Tell me about your family in Canada."

Ben smiled and launched into a detailed description. He was the youngest of two brothers and one sister. They were all married. One of them had kids. He was from a small town called Huntsville, a few hours north of Toronto, and he had grown up swimming in lakes during the summer and skating on ice during the winter. It sounded like he had a lovely family, and they were close too, from the way Ben spoke of them.

"What about your family?" Ben asked. It was an innocent question but, unfortunately for Sai, a painful one. His family was nothing like Ben's.

"My parents are retired. My father was a neurosurgeon, and my mother was a senior partner at a local real estate firm. We live up at the Peak."

"Neurosurgeon. Wow. That's really impressive."

"Yes, it is. Unfortunately he had to retire early due to arthritis."

"I'm sorry."

Sai shook his head at the apology. "Thank you. But he has managed to keep himself busy outside of the operating room."

"Yeah? What's he into?"

They passed the last sunbather on the beach, and a long expanse of sand stretched out before them. Ben spun around and walked backward, looking at Sai with heartfelt interest. How much of this he wanted to share? Many local Hong Kong-ers would recognize his father's name from the newspapers, and foreigners often treated him differently once they realized his parents were part of an elite group of influencers in the city. He had a feeling Ben wouldn't care, though.

"He dabbles in politics." Sai paused when Ben's eyes grew wide. "He's not a politician, but he's very vocal about his opinions in the news media."

"On what kind of issues?"

Sai scoffed. "Everything."

"But you don't agree with him."

Sai stopped walking and gazed out onto the vibrant blue water, their boat bobbing in the cove along with a handful of similar vessels. Disagree was an understatement. He couldn't count the number of times he had fumed in silence over some of the opinions his father held. His mother was only marginally better. She would just affix him with a stern look and remind him to respect his elders.

"No. Not on any of it." He continued walking, and Ben fell quietly into step beside him.

"You still live with your parents?" Ben asked.

He took a deep breath and pushed away thoughts of his father. "Yes." He glanced over to find Ben with an amused smile.

"I haven't lived with my parents since I moved away for university." He had one eyebrow cocked, and his lips curled in a grin. He was teasing, Sai could tell, from the way his eyes shone in the sunlight.

"In Hong Kong, it's rather common for unmarried children to remain living with their parents."

"Really? Even when you're an adult?" Ben asked, sounding incredulous.

Sai nodded.

"Does Winston live with his parents too?"

"No." Sai chuckled. The thought of Winston's parents putting up with his social life was amusing and also sad. "Winston lives with Jacques."

"That's not looked down upon?"

Sai's heart warmed at Ben's good questions. "It is looked down upon, but Winston is not one to stand on tradition."

"Why am I not surprised?"

He laughed out loud. Only a couple of encounters, and Ben already had such an accurate reading of Winston. Sai liked that about Ben, his attentiveness to his surroundings and his sincere desire to learn more. It made Ben all that more attractive to Sai. He couldn't wait to get Ben into his bed.

# 4

T HE RIDE back to Central Pier was long and quiet, and Sai slept for a good bit of it. He awoke to the lights of his city, blinking at them as they navigated through Victoria Harbour to the dock. The sight never failed to take his breath away—towering skyscrapers reaching up into the inky black of night, colored lights from both sides of the harbor battling for dominance and reflecting off the shimmering water.

"This is really cool." Ben tilted his head back to take in the scene.

"This is Hong Kong."

"You really love this place, eh?"

Sai turned to find Ben looking at him. "It's my home."

"You've never wanted to live anywhere else?"

Sai smiled. "Why would I want to live elsewhere when the whole world comes to me?"

Ben's chuckle rolled over Sai like a refreshing breath of air. The boat shook and bobbed as it docked, and the sudden movement brought them stumbling together. They grasped each other to steady themselves, the movement bringing them so close that mere inches separated their lips.

It would be so easy to lean in and learn what Ben's lips tasted like.

The shouts of the crew broke through their moment, and Sai stepped away to gather his things. They disembarked, and Sai waited as Ben and his friends discussed what to do next. When Ben turned to him with a suggestion for some new restaurant that had opened nearby, Sai adjusted his posture.

When he spoke, he dropped his voice. "Why don't I take you somewhere quiet, and then you can show me where you're staying."

Ben's Adam's apple bobbed, and his breath hitched. It took a split second for him to look over his shoulder and shout to Mo and the girls. "You guys go ahead. I'll catch you on Monday."

Sai didn't miss the knowing giggles from Ben's friends as they took off. He led Ben out to the street, and they jumped into the first cab they found. As the car pulled away from the curb, Ben's leg bounced up and down, his fingers knotted in his lap.

Sai reached over and put his hand on the bouncing knee with a firm grip, waiting until Ben met his eyes. He didn't say anything, just kept his grip firm, and after a couple of breaths, the nervous tension eased from Ben's body.

"I hope a simple dinner is okay with you." Sai spoke softly in the dim back seat of the cab.

"Uh, yeah, of course. What did you have in mind? I'm good with anything."

Ben was adorable when he was nervous.

"A local noodle place. It's easy and fast." He emphasized the last word with an extra squeeze of Ben's knee.

Ben's Adam's apple bobbed again, and he nodded. "Yeah, fast, that sounds good."

The ride was short, and Sai paid the driver before they

climbed out onto a small side street. He led the way to a brightly lit restaurant, glad to see that though it was busy, it wasn't so packed that they would have to wait for seats. The closer they came to actually getting into a bed, the less patience Sai had about getting there.

"Is there anything you want to eat in particular? Or anything you do not want?"

"Uh." Ben frowned at the menu posted on the wall, a useless exercise since it was all written in Chinese, but Sai waited with a smile until Ben gave up. "No, I'm good with anything."

"Perfect." Sai turned to the lady manning the little podium by the door and ordered two bowls of noodle soup and a couple plates of side dishes. Taking their receipt, he headed toward some empty seats at the far side of the restaurant and suppressed a laugh at the wide-eyed look on Ben's face.

"You haven't been to one of these places before?"

Ben shook his head, still looking around at the bare furnishings: long cheap-looking Formica tables surrounded by wobbly metal stools, and chopsticks and Chinese soup spoons stocked in worn hard plastic cutlery holders. Sai observed while Ben peeked over at the other customers and the food in their bowls.

It felt like seconds before their food arrived, just as fast as Sai hoped. Two bowls of steaming egg noodles in soup, topped with baby bok choy and giant wontons, a plate of blanched Chinese broccoli, and a plate of fried pancakes made of fish paste. Sai handed Ben a pair of chopsticks and a spoon, and dug in.

"Oh my God. This is so good," Ben mumbled around a mouthful of noodles. He swallowed and smiled sheepishly. "Sorry."

Sai grinned at the look of pleasure on Ben's face. It

seemed Ben enjoyed Chinese food, as if Sai needed yet another reason to be attracted to him. "I'm glad you like it. Eat, eat." He pushed the plate of greens toward Ben; they were going to need energy for what he had planned.

They devoured the food in less than ten minutes, and Sai practically dragged Ben out of the restaurant before he even swallowed his last bite. "You live on Hollywood Road, right?"

"Uh, yeah. That's in, um...." Ben swiveled his head around, a frown marring his forehead. But there was no need; Sai knew exactly where they needed to go.

"It's this way." Sai led them up several flights of stairs connecting parallel streets that ran along the side of a mountain.

"I never imagined Hong Kong would be this hilly," Ben huffed as he climbed up the last flight of stairs beside him.

"Hong Kong is basically a city built into a mountain." Sai paused. "This is Hollywood Road. Do you know where we are now?"

"Uh." Ben furrowed his brow before recognition set in. "Yes! I'm right there." He pointed across the street and down the block.

They took off in a jog toward Ben's building and were giggly and out of breath by the time they made it to the residents' door. Sai did his best to keep himself in check as Ben dug through his bag for his keys, but couldn't resist laying a hand across the small of Ben's back. As soon as they were inside the elevator and Ben had pressed the button for the twentieth floor, Sai pushed him back against the wall and reveled in the way Ben melted under his touch.

Their lips hovered just millimeters apart, and the scent of the sea on Ben's skin, mixed with the distinctive smell of the sun cream, filled Sai's senses. Ben's breath was hot as it blew across Sai's lips.

"Sai," Ben breathed, spoken in barely a whisper, and yet it echoed in Sai's ears. It sounded like surrender. It was delicious.

Sai closed the distance, crushing their lips together as Ben whimpered. The world faded away, and all that remained was that kiss: Ben's lips under his own, and Ben clutching at his shirt. Sai swiped his tongue across the seam of Ben's mouth and slipped inside when Ben opened for him. On the outside Ben might have appeared accommodating and meek, yet he was anything but when it came to kissing. He tangled his tongue with Sai's, making Sai's blood burn hot in his veins.

The elevator jerked to a stop, and the doors opened with a ding. Growling, Sai stepped back enough to let Ben off first, but then moved in close to nuzzle the back of Ben's neck. He growled again with satisfaction when Ben fumbled his key in distraction and dropped it on the floor.

When they finally got the door open, Sai all but pushed Ben inside and spun him around to press him against the nearest wall. He claimed Ben's mouth again—lips soft under his own, tongue dexterous as he swiped it against Sai's. Ben sure knew how to kiss, and Sai angled in to press deeper.

Sai pulled away only when he started feeling light-headed. They were both gasping for air, held upright by their hands clinging to each other. Sai hadn't felt this way in a long time, the unstoppable rush of desire that tore away at his control and consumed him from the inside out. With shaking limbs, he forced himself to put a little distance between them.

Ben's eyes were half-open, the blue of his irises barely visible behind his blown pupils. His lips were swollen and red from their kisses, and when he pulled his bottom lip between his teeth, the last of Sai's self-control slipped away.

"Bed," Sai growled.

He kept a hand on Ben's arm as Ben pushed off the wall with unsteady feet. It only took a few steps before they stood next to the bed that dominated the small studio apartment.

"Strip," Sai commanded.

Ben gasped, but he obeyed without hesitation. His movements didn't appear deliberately sexy or intended to tease. But the slow unveiling of his body and the way he kept his gaze steady on Sai made Sai's cock thicken and pulse. The striptease stalled with Ben's thumbs hooked in the waistband of his swim shorts, pulled low enough to reveal several curls of pubic hair.

He had nothing on underneath, Sai realized. "Do it," Sai breathed.

He pushed his shorts down in excruciatingly slow motion; his hard dick slapped up against his stomach as he kicked the last of his clothes away. Naked, he ducked his head and dropped his gaze to the floor, and Sai drew in a sharp inhale at the bashful movement.

Sai closed the distance between them. With one hand, he cupped Ben's face, palm against his cheek. Ben turned into the touch, and his eyes fluttered closed. His stubble, almost invisible in its blondness, scratched at Sai's fingers, reminding Sai that despite Ben's youthful features and innocent exuberance, this was a man standing before him.

Sai lifted his other hand and drew it lightly down Ben's chest, remembering the heat of Ben's skin under his fingers as he applied the sun cream that morning. Had that just been a mere eight hours ago? It felt like a lifetime.

Ben's chest hair was soft, almost downy, growing thicker as it ran down the middle of his stomach. Sai's first contact with Ben's cock was brief, just a light swipe of his thumb over the top to collect the bead of precome gathering there. He brought his thumb up to Ben's mouth, and Ben moaned as he sucked it inside. Ben's tongue felt rough as he twirled it around like he was sucking on a dick instead of a finger.

Sai yanked his hand away and replaced his thumb with his tongue. Ben's moans were music to his ears. Sai let his hands roam down Ben's neck and across his shoulders, down his back until they were filled with the plump muscles of Ben's ass. He squeezed—hard.

How was it a man could feel like hard steel and soft silk in his arms at the same time? Sai pulled him close and thrilled at the way Ben molded to him like an elegant, draping fabric. Sai's dick was hard, his pulse raced, and he couldn't wait to be inside this beautiful enigma of a man.

Sai gave Ben a shove, and he landed with a bounce on the bed. Without needing to be told, Ben shuffled backward until he propped himself up on a pillow. Now it was Sai's turn to strip, and he did so swiftly, with none of the slow hesitation that had been Ben's striptease. Naked, Sai crawled up on his hands and knees, never once taking his eyes off the dazed look on Ben's face.

When he was close enough to reach it, Sai grabbed the pillow from behind Ben's head and yanked it out. Ben dropped down with a ragged breath and a shudder. Sai captured Ben's mouth again in a kiss—he was quickly becoming addicted to those kisses—and with his knees, he pushed Ben's legs wide.

Sai savored the feeling of Ben's hands on him, digging those fingers into his flesh, trying to pull him closer. But when he lowered his weight onto Ben, he grasped Ben's hands and pinned them above Ben's head. The desperate whine and the way Ben arched up into him only served to fuel Sai's desire.

Sai broke the kiss to utter one word. "Condoms."

"Drawer." Ben's voice was thick with lust. "Under the bed."

Sai released Ben's hands, and Ben twisted to reach for the necessary supplies.

"Put it on me." Sai sat back on his heels, hands on Ben's thighs, holding him in place.

Sai barely restrained his need as Ben tore at the foiled packet with trembling hands; it took him several tries to rip the packet open far enough to get the condom out. The first touch of Ben's fingers on his cock was pure pleasure, but he kept himself still for Ben's slow unrolling of the condom on his dick. He tightened his grip on Ben's thighs and would probably leave marks, but Sai didn't care. He wanted to leave his mark on him; he wanted to make Ben his.

He grabbed Ben's wrists as soon as the condom was in place and brought them up over Ben's head again. Ben gasped as Sai pressed him down into the mattress.

"Don't move them," Sai ordered.

"Yes...," Ben breathed, and when Sai let go, Ben wrapped his fingers around the bar of the headboard.

Satisfaction curled in Sai's chest at Ben's obedience.

He took the bottle of lube lying next to them and coated his cock and fingers with the cool gel. Then he pushed Ben's legs up until Ben's knees were practically in his armpits and his hole was on display. What a beautiful sight.

Sai traced the wrinkled skin and then gently pushed a finger inside. Ben's hissed yes was more than enough encouragement for Sai to increase his speed, twisting and curling his finger until Ben was wiggling his ass back and forth in need.

"Sai, please."

"Please what?" Sai brushed his finger against Ben's prostate.

Ben arched off the bed with a cry, and Sai pushed him down with a hand to the back of a knee.

"Please fuck me, Sai. Please?"

A smile graced Sai's lips at Ben's begging, voice raised several tones, laced with an unmistakable desire to be taken. Sai fed himself into Ben's ass inch by sweet, mind-blowing inch. When he bottomed out, they both trembled, and Sai knew there was no way this would last long. Sai braced himself against the back of Ben's knees, pinning him down so he couldn't move, and started fucking him.

It was fast and hard, the sound of skin slapping against skin filling the air around them, mixing with the incoherent moans escaping Ben's throat. One of Ben's hands slipped from its hold on the headboard as he reached for his cock. Sai caught Ben's hand halfway and pinned it to the mattress.

"No touching," he growled as Ben shook under him. "Not until I say you can."

Ben whimpered and bit his rosy bottom lip. His cries grew louder as the fucking got harder, but to Sai's joy, he didn't try to touch his cock again. He took every inch Sai gave him with tremors and gasps and some skilled working of his ass muscles. Sai's dick was getting milked, his come coaxed out of him, not just by Ben's succulent ass, but also by the fucked-out look on Ben's face, the way Ben's knuckles turned white, and his blond hair plastered to his skin with sweat.

Sai exploded into the condom with little warning, his climax taking him as Ben whispered his name. Sai's ears rang and he saw spots, and when he pushed himself up from where he'd collapsed on top of Ben, Ben still had his hands above his head, dick hard and leaking. He lay there, a tightly wound ball of arousal, and Sai took a moment to soak in the pleasure of having such a man under him.

He slowly lowered Ben's legs and ran his hands over the thickness of Ben's thighs and stomach. Ben's cock jerked as Sai raked his fingernails lightly down his chest and abdomen.

"Please, Sai. I need to come."

"Do you?" Sai loved dragging this out, making Ben beg.

"Yes, please. Please let me come." Ben's voice broke as he tilted his hips up. Sai pushed them back down and then took pity on him.

Ben let out a strangled cry as Sai wrapped his hand around Ben's dick. The veins stood out in sharp relief, the head red and engorged. Sai ran his hand up, then down, then released it to cup Ben's heavy balls. He rolled them in his palm and felt them pull up toward Ben's body.

Sai trailed his gaze back up Ben's sweat-slicked body to find blown blue eyes staring back at him, his bottom lip caught between his teeth. Sai maintained the eye contact as he flicked out his tongue to swipe at the tip of Ben's cock. Then he took it into his mouth, tasting Ben's precome, salty like the seawater. He sank down on Ben's dick, using his tongue and his throat muscles to work it over.

"Oh God, Sai." Ben's cries were beautiful.

Ben bucked once, but Sai pushed him back down with a hand clamped on a hip and eyes narrowed in admonition. A whimper escaped, but Ben held still. Sai bobbed, moaning around the thickness of Ben in his mouth and throat. Ben was primed to come, nearly vibrating with the need. And all it took was a couple of fingers slipped inside his used hole and a couple of taps on his prostate, and Sai was swallowing all the salty come that shot onto his tongue.

Holding Ben afterward felt like he had acquired a new addiction. As the sweat cooled on their skin and Sai pulled the covers over them to protect against the breeze of the air-conditioning, he knew this one time would never be enough.

5

S unday, September 10

THE TABLE was covered in little plates and bamboo steaming baskets, the aroma making Ben's mouth water. He'd been to dim sum a couple of times before in Toronto; some of his Chinese friends had taken him. They would order a bunch of things he had never heard of, and everything looked strangely appetizing when it arrived. It was no different this time around with Sai, Winston, and Jacques sitting at the table with him.

It was on the tip of his tongue to ask what everything was, but Ben held back. The last thing he wanted was to seem like the uneducated gweilo who needed handholding when eating dim sum. Jacques certainly didn't look like he needed anything explained to him as he picked up a pair of chopsticks and expertly snagged some sort of dumpling.

"Okay." Next to him Sai used his chopsticks to point from one dish to the next. "These are barbecue pork buns, baked instead of steamed, which is a specialty at this restau-

44

rant. This is shrimp dumplings, pork dumplings, radish cake, deep-fried taro dumplings with pork inside, rolled noodles with shrimp inside, glutinous rice with chicken, satay snow pea sprouts, and congee with pork and thousand-year-old egg."

Ben's head spun. "Thousand-year-old egg?" It was honestly the only thing he could remember after Sai rambled off the items on their table.

"Yes, it's black and looks rubbery. It's delicious." Sai ladled some into his bowl and picked out a piece on his spoon.

It did look rubbery and black, and what looked to be the yolk was mushy and gray. His reaction must have been written across his face because Sai, Winston, and Jacques all burst out laughing at the same time. The heat of a blush burned on his ears; so much for not being an uneducated gweilo.

"Don't worry!" Winston waved at him from across the table. "It's good! Try it!"

Ben gulped. He told himself he was open and adventurous, and so far he hadn't encountered anything in Hong Kong he wasn't willing to try. Nothing except perhaps a thousand-year-old egg.

"You don't have to try it if you don't want to." Sai shot Winston a glare. "It's just a normal chicken egg that's been preserved in some clay or something—I'm not too sure. But it's not a thousand years old." Sai put his bowl down and picked up his chopsticks again.

"No, I'll try it." And he nodded to prove to himself and the other three that he meant it. "I mean, that's what I'm here for, right? To try new things?"

They all looked at him like they didn't believe him. Well, he'd show them. He snatched the bowl Sai had abandoned and scooped up the black rubbery thing with the

Chinese soup spoon. It was cut up into small pieces and sitting in the congee that looked like rice porridge. It couldn't be that bad, right? Not when an entire culture of people ate the stuff. Ben held his breath and put it in his mouth.

The yolk was as mushy as it looked and disintegrated on his tongue. The white was jiggly like Jell-O, and he gave it a couple of chews before swallowing. It tasted tangy and slightly pickled and reminded Ben of the smell of an extinguished match. It wasn't as gross as it looked, but it probably wouldn't become Ben's favorite go-to.

Three pairs of eyes looked expectantly at him.

He shrugged. "It's okay."

They burst out laughing again.

Jacques shook his head as he turned back to his own food. "Don't let them fool you. Most non-Chinese don't like that stuff. I never eat it."

"Because you have bad taste in food," Winston accused him with a dramatic eye.

Jacques tilted his chin up and looked down his nose. "I'm French," he said with an accent slightly heavier than it was a second ago. "I have the best taste in food."

"Ignore them." Sai's chopsticks clicked as his hand flew around the table.

When Ben finally figured out what Sai was doing, he found his plate piled high with a sample of everything they had ordered.

"Oh, thanks. You didn't have to do that." He picked up his own chopsticks and tried to decide what he wanted first.

"It's a sign of respect to get food for others." The way Sai smiled at him, dark and suggestive, reminded Ben of all the things they had done together the night before. His ass still ached from the pounding Sai had given him, but he would gladly take it again at the crook of Sai's finger.

"You can stop eye-fucking now," Winston said with his heavy Cantonese accent and a dismissive tone.

He almost laughed out loud at how annoyed Winston looked. When he glanced over to Sai, his smile had turned smug, and Ben's blush deepened.

"So, Ben. How long have you been in Hong Kong for now?" Jacques came to the rescue with a much-needed change of subject.

"Um." Ben paused to think. "Just over a week," he answered, although it felt so much longer than that.

"What has been your favorite part so far?" Jacques asked and took a sip of his tea.

Sai—the answer rang out as clear as if someone has spoken it in Ben's ear. But as he glanced at the man in question, who was busy dipping a dumpling in chili oil, he knew he couldn't say his answer out loud.

"The people," Ben said instead. "Everyone has been so nice and welcoming to me."

Three pairs of eyes stared at him again, and Ben wondered what he had said wrong.

"Truly?" Jacques looked surprised.

"Yeah, I mean. Look at you guys, inviting me for dim sum even though you just met me." And it was true. They didn't make him feel like a foreigner or an outsider; they just seemed to accept him into the fold.

The same went for the people at work. Granted, now that he thought about it, most of the people he interacted with at work were also expats. The locals seemed to keep to themselves.

"We are an exception," Jacques went on. "I'm a moderator for InterNations—"

"Right—you guys put on that networking event."

Jacques nodded. "Exactly. Our mission is to connect expats and make them feel welcome in new cities. So we're extra welcoming. Locals, though, don't have the greatest reputation."

Winston gave his boyfriend an annoyed look but didn't dispute the statement. Sai popped a piece of radish cake in his mouth and chewed, seemingly indifferent to Jacques's slight.

"Kwok Sai Hei?"

Sai looked up, and Ben followed his gaze to find an older couple standing a few steps away from their table. Sai jumped from his seat, switching to rapid Cantonese as he addressed them. Winston lost all his typical energy, his expression grim and somber as he stood less quickly and went over to say hello.

Ben leaned over to Jacques and whispered, "Who are they?"

Jacques turned toward Ben and lowered his voice. "They're the Leungs. Friends of Winston and Sai's parents. They own several factories, and Sai acts as legal counsel for them. They're an influential family, but then, they're all influential."

"They?"

"Winston and Sai's families. They're from an elite social circle in Hong Kong. Mostly business people, but active in politics."

"Oh." Ben hesitated. "Should we introduce ourselves?"

Jacques gave a curt shake of his head. "No. We are not important gwaanhai—connections. We're not in positions that are useful for their network, so there's no reason for them to want to know us. Also they're a little homophobic." Jacques shrugged and tore a BBQ pork bun in half.

Ben glanced at the older couple. The woman had her hands clasped tightly in front of her, her chin lifted, and she looked at Sai with haughty annoyance. The man stood just behind her, off to the side, scowling not too subtly at Winston. Winston scowled not so subtly back.

Sai nodded at everything the woman said, his nods only deepening when it was his turn to speak. Ben couldn't understand a word of the conversation, but he didn't need to understand the language to read the power dynamic at play.

The woman's gaze shot to their table, first to Ben, then to Jacques, so quickly that Ben didn't have time to smile at her before she turned on her heel and marched away. The man followed after a shake of his head.

Winston returned to the table with his back ramrod straight, vibrating with a barely contained fury. Sai sat down in a slump, elbow landing heavy on the table, forehead cradled in his palm. Ben covered Sai's other hand with his own, but he wasn't prepared for the way Sai jerked his hand away and busied himself with his cloth napkin.

The mood changed dramatically. Jacques tried to keep the conversation lively, and Ben did his best to contribute. But Sai and Winston were clearly distracted by whatever went down in that exchange. When Ben shot a worried look at Jacques, he just got another curt shake of the head and more forced chitchat.

The food still tasted good, but it wasn't nearly as enjoyable as it had been. The current of tension at the table eased only when the waiter brought over their bill. Ben pulled out his wallet, but Sai pushed his hand away and started in on a rapid-fire discussion with Winston in Cantonese.

When Ben glanced over at Jacques in confusion, Jacques just shrugged.

"They're arguing over the bill," he explained when Winston and Sai continued their argument at the restaurant's reception desk.

"Why? We should all split it."

"Oh no!" Jacques gave him a mockingly horrified look.

"That is unacceptable. They must fight over who pays, and the person who wins is considered the most generous and hospitable." Jacques paused with an amused smile. "Winston and Sai aren't so bad, really. Others often resort to extreme measures."

"To pay for the meal?" Ben couldn't quite believe it.

"Oh, certainly. It's very amusing to watch people trying to sneak cash into each other's pockets," Jacques said as they left the restaurant.

Winston and Sai met them outside, and after a quick goodbye, Winston and Jacques left to run some errands.

"Thanks for taking me to dim sum," Ben said.

"It was my pleasure." Sai's smile held a hint of sadness, and his shoulders slumped in a way Ben had never seen before. "And I apologize for that... incident."

"No! Don't apologize! I just hope everything's okay."

Sai's smile slipped. "They're friends of my parents. And Winston's parents."

"Right, Jacques told me who they were. They were nice to come by and say hello."

Sai gave a dry chuckle. "It would've been rude if they did not. They wouldn't want to risk rumors getting around that they failed to uphold basic social pleasantries." Sai paused, lips pressed in a firm line. "Even if we are gay."

Ben's mouth gaped, and he snapped it shut; it appeared Jacques had been right about the homophobic thing. But before Ben could conjure up any response, Sai put a hand on his shoulder, warm, solid.

"I'm sorry, Ben," Sai said with a hint of sadness. "I had wanted to take you to the Kowloon side this afternoon, but I need to go in to the office now."

"Oh, yeah. It's okay." Ben tried to hide his disappointment but couldn't stop his brow from wrinkling. "Does it have anything to do with the couple?"

Sai narrowed his eyes, and Ben could almost see him debate with himself before he finally spoke. "Yes, but it's... nothing."

Said that way, Ben didn't believe for a second it was nothing. "Are you sure everything's okay?"

Sai sighed and dropped his hand from Ben's shoulder. "I act as legal counsel for the Leungs, and they just told me that a new issue has come up, so I need to go address it immediately. Don't worry; this happens a lot. I'm used to it."

It might happen a lot, but to Ben, that didn't make it okay, even if Sai was used to it. It was on the tip of his tongue to say something, but what did he know about the dynamics of Sai's relationship with the Leungs? Hell, for all he knew, this could be normal for Hong Kong.

"Okay, well, next time?" If he sounded a little desperate, Ben didn't care.

Sai met his gaze and held it for several seconds. "Yes, next time." A small grin graced Sai's lips. "Definitely next time."

6

———

*S*aturday, September 16

BEN CHECKED his watch again as he waited at the lower terminal of the tram that would take them up to the Peak, the tallest part of Hong Kong island. Sai was twenty minutes late. Ben had already texted Sai where he was waiting but hadn't gotten a response.

He reached into his pocket to pull out his phone again but stopped when he spotted Sai striding toward him, head bent, shoulders drooping, one hand stuffed into his jeans pocket, the other clutching the strap of a messenger bag slung across his chest. This did not look like the confidently suave Sai Ben had come to expect.

"Hey, Sai," Ben said as Sai strode up.

"Hi, Ben." The smile Sai gave him looked genuine, if labored.

"Are you okay?"

His smiled tightened a little around the edges, and Sai

looked away as if he couldn't meet Ben's gaze. "Yeah, I'm okay. I'm fine."

Ben frowned. "Are you sure? You don't look okay. Did something happen?"

Sai's smile slipped a little more, as if plastered on his face by sheer will. "Yeah, fine. It's fine. Let's get in the queue." Sai gestured toward the line that snaked back and forth across the lobby. He started off without waiting, and Ben scrambled to keep up.

"How was your day?" Sai asked.

Sai had completely ignored his question, but Ben let it go for now. "Um, yeah, it was good. Slept in and then met up with Mo and the girls for lunch. We wandered around Wan Chai for a bit."

Sai nodded and made appropriate sounds of agreement, but Ben wondered if he'd actually been listening.

"Did you go in to work?" Ben asked.

More nodding, but Sai didn't offer up any details. "There's quite a history to the Peak. At one point only expats were allowed to live up there."

Ben was torn between the interesting piece of history and the fact that Sai had again acted as if Ben hadn't asked a question. "Oh, really? That's crazy."

Sai shrugged dismissively. "British colonialism. Back then the only way to get up to the Peak was by foot. The tram wasn't built until 1888."

The line moved quickly, and Sai spouted an unending stream of historical facts about the tram and the mountain they were going to see. Ben let him talk. It was interesting information, but more than that, it seemed to take Sai's mind off whatever was clearly bothering him. By the time they got to the front, a bit of the tension had eased from Sai's posture, and his smile looked a little less forced.

Ben managed to snag a window seat on their tram, and Sai slid in next to him, resting his arm along the back of the bench. It felt nice, sitting on the bench so narrow they had no choice but to touch thighs, arms, and shoulders. Ben slouched as far down as the small space would allow, leaning on Sai's shoulder.

As the tram climbed up through residential neighborhoods, with trees, shrubbery, and vines encroaching on the tracks, Sai pointed out landmarks of interest. Ben soaked it all in, every little piece of information spoken in hushed tones in his ear. Sai might have been smaller in stature, but in that moment, he felt so much bigger to Ben, so sure and in control.

The air got marginally cooler the higher up they ascended, helped by the canopy of vegetation and the slight breeze. When they got to the top, Ben was pleased to see Sai visibly more relaxed, as if by physically going up the mountain, he left behind all the troubles that lay below.

The sun was low in the sky as they made their way into the Peak Tower, a bowl-shaped building set on a pedestal. Inside was a giant shopping mall, but Ben followed Sai to the elevators that brought them to the viewing deck. The sight was stunning.

Hong Kong was laid out at their feet, towering buildings growing out of thick green vegetation, all clinging to the side of a mountain that gave way to the sea. On the other side of Victoria Harbour was Kowloon and more towering skyscrapers, each reaching for the heavens in their attempt to be the tallest of their peers. And beyond them, more mountains covered in green.

This was Hong Kong: a battle between the concrete structures of modernity and the stubborn resiliency of nature. Urban centers so densely populated that people lived and worked on top of each other, juxtaposed with untouched landscapes that spanned as far as the eye could see.

"It's beautiful," Ben whispered. It wasn't like anything he'd seen before, and something in his heart shifted. All around them were shouting tourists snapping pictures, but Ben felt oddly tranquil standing on top of the mountain. Hong Kong wasn't home for him, but he could see it becoming something like home.

"It is."

Ben dragged his gaze away from the scene below and found Sai looking at him—eyes dark, lips pressed in a firm line. Ben's stomach fluttered, and his mouth grew dry. He slipped into that place again. There were no words to describe it, and he didn't fully understand it, but with that place came a sense of relief, of being able to let go of the reins of control he normally held on to so tightly. He swayed closer to Sai, and Sai swayed a little closer to him.

Just when Ben was sure they'd meet in a kiss, Sai pulled back with a frown. He dropped his gaze as he pulled out his phone, and the ringing Ben had subconsciously ignored grew louder. Sai threw him a quick apologetic smile and answered it.

"Wei?" he answered in Cantonese as his frown deepened.

Ben turned back to the view and tried to enjoy it, even as Sai's one-word answers became more and more curt. He seemed angry. But Ben couldn't tell whether that was the sound of the language, or if the eye rolls, shifting feet, and barely audible sighs meant the same thing in English as they did in Chinese.

Sai hung up, and Ben wasn't sure if he heard the words for goodbye before Sai removed the phone from his ear and glared at it.

"Is everything okay?" Ben asked.

"That was my father." Which wasn't really an answer, at least not one Ben understood.

"What did he want?"

Sai kept glaring at his phone, head bowed, lips pressed so tightly together it was as if he was trying to keep something vile from spilling out of his mouth.

"Sai?"

His head shot up as if he'd forgotten Ben was even there.

"What's wrong?" It was so obvious. Ben couldn't just keep on ignoring it.

Sai let out a heavy sigh through his nose. Then took a deep breath and did it again. "It's my father." His voice was tight, barely restrained. "He's being... unreasonable."

Ben cocked his head. He had a feeling "unreasonable" was a euphemism for something much worse. If he had learned anything in his two weeks in Hong Kong, it was the Chinese people's ability to understate everything.

"Unreasonable?"

Sai gave him a hard look, dark eyes searching for something in Ben's expression. Perhaps something to indicate he could trust Ben with whatever was bothering him. What did a trustworthy expression look like? Ben had no idea. But he tried his best—nonthreatening, nonjudgmental, positive and open vibes all around.

Sai blinked, and the examination was over. But the sad smile that graced his lips and the small shake of his head signaled Ben wasn't going to get the answers he itched for. "It's a long story for another time."

What could he say? It wasn't his place to intrude.

"Look, the sun's setting." There Sai went again, changing the subject.

Was it a Chinese thing to avoid talking about things? Or just a Sai thing? Maybe he could ask Jacques and Winston about it.

Ben turned back to the view. Orange light shone across the sky and illuminated all the glass-covered buildings until the whole city glowed as if it were on fire. It was spectacular. There was no denying that.

Next to Ben, Sai shifted and their shoulders brushed before Sai pressed firmly against him. They stood together as the sun set, the orange fire fading almost as quickly as it had flared. As the city descended into darkness, the buildings took on a life of their own, lit by a rainbow of colored lights. Down by the harbor, a light show began, with lasers tracing patterns in the sky and images projected onto the sides of buildings.

It almost didn't look real to Ben, more like something he'd see in a movie than with his own eyes. If he were honest, very little of the past two weeks felt real. Riding a wave of adrenaline, boosted by jet lag, every new experience felt like the best thing he'd ever encountered—Sai included.

Their time together so far had been like a dream. Something just clicked when they were sharing the same space, like they could slip into roles written specifically for them, roles that brought out their true selves. Ben had never felt that way with anyone before, not even with his family, and certainly never with any of his ex-boyfriends.

He hoped this connection wasn't some figment of his overactive imagination, him seeing something that wasn't there because of how much he liked Sai. It would be hard, he realized, if this whole thing turned out to be a one-sided relationship conjured out of nothing more than a couple of casual dates and a quick fuck. He was probably already more invested than was healthy. After all, he was leaving at the end of his three-month stint, so even if this was a relationship, where could it realistically go?

For the first time in his life, the answer wasn't immediately clear. He'd been lucky in the past, Ben knew. Most of his important life decisions had come easily: where he went to school, what he wanted to study, career choices, and even former relationships, everything tended to fall into place without too much trouble. But this thing with Sai? It made him want things he didn't know he wanted, made him second-guess himself and pushed him outside of what was comfortable.

"Ready to go?" Sai asked.

Not really. Sai's hot-and-cold behavior today was a bucket of cold water on Ben's little honeymoon phase. A part of himself wanted to hit the pause button before real life started rolling in. Standing at the top of the world felt safe.

He sighed. "Yeah, okay."

They took the tram back down the mountain and then jumped into a cab. Sai rattled off some instructions in Cantonese, and the cab took off in a lurch that had Ben bracing himself. The ride itself didn't take long, and they soon stopped at a familiar street corner, the same one they had gone to after the horse race. All the restaurants had their sliding doors pulled back, and people loitered out on the street, holding glasses and bottles of alcohol.

Ben blinked in surprise when Sai grabbed his hand. But Sai just smiled, eyes dark, lips tilting with amusement, and led the way into the fray.

# 7

$S$AI AND Winston were in a heated argument. At least that's what it looked like from where Ben stood, pretending to chat with Jacques. Winston looked annoyed, with his arms crossed over his chest and an eyebrow arched so high Ben thought it might climb off his forehead. Sai scowled, stabbing angrily at the air and shaking his head. He had downed his gin and tonic almost as soon as he got it and was now waving the empty glass around so much that Ben was afraid he might drop it.

He noticed belatedly Jacques had stopped talking and followed the direction of Ben's gaze to where Sai and Winston were arguing.

Jacques shook his head. "They do that every so often."

"Argue like that? It looks heated."

"Well, Cantonese is a heated language. But judging from Winston's body language, they're arguing about Sai's job again." Jacques spun around so he stood next to Ben, both watching the confrontation go down.

"Sai's job?" Ben glanced over at Jacques, who nodded. "What about it?"

Jacques opened his mouth as if to speak, but then stopped short and snapped it shut.

"What?" Ben frowned. He probably shouldn't push the issue, but curiosity got the better of him.

Jacques hemmed and hawed before giving in. "Most of Sai's job is representing the friends of his parents—wealthy business people like the Leungs. He often gets asked to do... things he'd rather not do."

"What does that mean?"

Jacques cast one last glance at Sai and Winston before turning around and lowering his voice. "Listen, it's all over the news anyway, if you want to look it up." He sighed. "The Leungs have a reputation for, ah... less-than-ethical treatment of their employees. There was an exposé in the newspaper a couple of years ago, and since then, they've been the targets of protests by human rights activists. There was one this past week. It was big. People were arrested. Whenever stuff like this happens, and it tends to happen regularly, Sai is called in to do damage control."

"Oh." Ben wasn't sure how to interpret this new information. "And he's okay with that?"

Jacques looked at him with a surprised expression. "No. Of course he's not okay with that. He'd probably go and represent the protestors in court if he wasn't already on the other side of the issue."

Jacques paused and eyed Ben for so long that Ben wondered what he had missed. "You know that Sai is one of those bleeding-heart liberals, right? He went down and joined all those student demonstrators a few years ago when they were protesting Beijing's influence in local politics. He got in so much trouble with his father because of it."

"Oh." Ben was confused. Why would Sai work for people he disagreed with?

Jacques sighed, heavy and despondent. "The Chinese

are great people, but there are some things I will never understand."

"What kinds of things?" Ben asked.

"This argument that Winston and Sai are having?" Jacques nodded toward their friends.

Sai looked calmer now, if more defeated with his head hanging low. His glass had disappeared, and he stood with both hands on his hips. Winston shook his head as he spoke.

"I can't count the number of times they've had this argument," Jacques said. "It's always the same: Sai complains about what the Leungs—or one of his other clients—are asking him to do; Winston tells him he needs to quit. But Sai doesn't think he can quit because of some ridiculous edict his father handed down about what he must do with his life. Winston berates him for being too traditional, and then Sai storms off. Wait, watch, we're almost there."

And sure enough, as they stood and watched, Sai threw a hand in the air, spun on his heel, and marched back into the bar, leaving Winston on the street shaking his head. After a moment, Winston turned toward them and caught Ben's gaze. There was something in that look Winston gave him that made Ben feel like an outsider, like he had intruded into their lives, and Winston wasn't sure whether he could be trusted.

Ben dropped his gaze to the beer he was nursing. Who was he kidding? He was an outsider. What right did he have to have an opinion on Sai's life?

He didn't notice Winston come over until Jacques spoke.

"Same old argument?" Jacques asked.

"Mostly," Winston said and gave Ben a penetrating look. "For how much longer are you in Hong Kong, Ben?"

Ben did a bit of mental math. "Two and a half months still. Why?"

Winston didn't answer right away, his normal exuberance so tempered that Ben worried that something bad had happened. Then he smiled—a little contrived—and turned to his boyfriend. "I need another drink."

Winston and Jacques disappeared inside, leaving Ben to ponder what he had just witnessed. Winston hadn't said it out loud, but his meaning was clear—Ben was only there temporarily. The issues surrounding Sai and his job were longstanding, and Ben was just a blip in the timeline. What place did he really have in all of it? None.

His glass was empty, and like Winston, he needed another drink. Pushing his way through the other customers, he found Sai still at the bar. "Hey."

Sai glanced at him, and for a moment, Ben could see all the weariness Sai carried inside, the heaviness of the burden and the frustration that came with living another person's agenda—it was all written plain as day on Sai's face. Then Sai hung his head, and when he lifted it again, all that emotion was gone. Back was the reserved but charming man who'd caught Ben's imagination and wouldn't let go.

Ben's heart skipped a beat when Sai straightened and lifted his head. The changes were so subtle that Ben couldn't pinpoint what exactly they were, but all together, it turned Sai into a figure Ben could never say no to.

"See? There it is again."

Ben barely heard the words, but his subconscious mind labeled the voice as Winston's.

"Are you seeing this? It's so ridiculous."

"Yes, babe. I see it." That was Jacques.

"Hello? We're right here!"

Ben ignored them because Sai ignored them. And the way Sai was looking at him now, there wasn't any way Ben could turn away, even if he wanted to. Sai slipped his hand over his—the simple touch warmed Ben's heart—and they pushed through the throng of people until they found a cozy little spot on the dance floor.

The music was good, electronic dance music mixed in with the latest top-forty pop songs in a variety of languages. When Sai smiled at him, teasing with a dark look in his eyes, Ben couldn't help but move to the beat thrumming through him. He draped his arms around Sai's shoulders and shuffled closer when Sai wrapped his hands around his lower back.

All the unanswered questions about Sai fled to the back of Ben's mind, unimportant as he stood in his arms. All Ben knew was there was something inside Sai that called out to him and drew him in with such intensity his head reeled.

They danced all night, stopping for drinks and then dancing some more. Sai might not have been great at dancing, but he was a master at standing there with desire in his eyes, driving Ben to move his body until they were both panting with lust. By the time they got back to Ben's apartment, he'd all but forgotten about Sai's moodiness from earlier, the strange call from Sai's father, and Jacques's comments.

Too bad that didn't seem to be the case with Sai. He dropped onto the little love seat in Ben's apartment, staring off into the distance. Ben got them each a glass of water and squeezed himself onto the sofa next to Sai.

"What's wrong?" Ben couldn't ignore it anymore; he didn't want to ignore it. Maybe this was only a three-month fling, but he wasn't the type to just take what he wanted from a relationship and leave the other person to fend for themselves.

Sai looked like he was about to deflect again, but Ben squeezed his hand. "Tell me. What's wrong? Is it the Leungs?"

Sai's brows lowered. "What do you know about the

Leungs?"

"Jacques mentioned them."

Sai shut his eyes and pressed his lips into a thin line. "Fucking Jacques. He never knows when to shut up."

"Sorry." Maybe Ben should have left that part out.

"Don't be sorry." Sai squeezed his hand. "It's all out there, anyway. The Leungs aren't the greatest people."

Ben let out the question that had been bothering him from earlier. "So why do you still work for them?"

Sai shifted as if Ben's question had hit him with physical force. "It's not so easy. I can't just quit."

"Why not? No—" Ben straightened when Sai started to protest. "Explain it to me. I want to understand."

Sai did that examining thing again where he looked at Ben with assessing eyes, as if weighing how much he should share.

"You can tell me." Ben shifted closer. "I mean, as much as you're allowed to tell me. I'm good at listening."

It took another second before Sai sighed, and Ben knew he had won.

"Mark and Constance Leung. They have a daughter and a son who grew up with me and Winston. They are close friends with my parents. Uncle Mark and my father go golfing all the time. They own a manufacturing firm with some factories in Hong Kong. If you look them up, you'll probably find an old article about the poor working conditions in those factories from years ago." Sai shook his head, a frown marring his brow.

"I worked with them to change things in the months after that article was published. We made really good headway. Conditions were improving, and we had labor department inspectors come in and do assessments. There were still protestors." Sai shrugged. "They had a right to protest. Things were far from ideal."

Sai paused as if debating what he should say next. "Things were better for a while. But as with all things, people backslide."

"So conditions are bad again?"

Sai winced. "To say they were ever really good is misleading."

"Why can't you keep pressuring them to change? I mean, you're their legal counsel. Your word must mean something."

The laugh that escaped Sai's throat was anything but amused. "I may be their legal counsel, but I'm also the son of a friend. I call them Uncle and Auntie to show them respect. They have no reason to listen to what I have to say."

"But you're the legal expert."

"You flatter me, Ben. I may be a legal expert to you. But to them I'm just a child with a law degree who can sign their papers and be their mouthpiece to the media."

Ben gaped. Put that way, Sai's job sounded really crude. But to a certain extent, Ben could understand. He had friends whose parents still treated them like children even though they were all adults.

"It's okay if you don't understand, Ben. It's one of those Chinese things that doesn't always make much sense to foreigners. But that's the way things are here." He smiled sardonically.

"No, I understand. But that doesn't make it okay." Ben frowned. "There has to be a way out; why can't you just quit?"

"I've tried before." There was that unamused laugh again. "But they won't accept my resignation."

"Probably because they wouldn't be able find another lawyer who'll bend the rules for them." Ben spat the words before he fully formed the idea. The brief glimmer of pain in Sai's eyes before he shut it down sliced through Ben as he realized what he had said. "Shit. No. I didn't mean to say that you'd bend the rules for them or anything like that."

"It's okay." Sai squeezed his hand. "I do bend the rules for them."

"But you don't want to!" Ben jumped to Sai's defense.

"True. But I still do it."

And the facts stood between them, as immovable as the mountain they'd visited earlier that day.

"What was that thing with your dad?" Ben asked.

"The phone call?"

When Ben nodded, Sai winced. "He wanted me to fix a situation."

"The situation with the Leungs?"

"Yes. There was a big demonstration at one of their factories last week, and several protestors were arrested. They were let out on bail, and, well, not everyone was happy about that." Sai shook his head and sighed. "They just don't understand. These people are allowed to protest. Maybe they crossed some lines, but going after them is only making the firm look worse than it already does.

"And my father getting involved is…. He shouldn't even know the things he does. He's not covered under our confidentiality umbrella, so they would have had to break attorney-client privilege for him to know all those details. If the defendants' legal team found out, we wouldn't even have a case to argue."

He stopped and slumped over, bracing his elbows on his knees. Ben shifted closer, pressing himself along Sai's back and slipping one hand around to hug Sai's waist. Sai put his hand over top of Ben's and squeezed it. Ben hugged him back tighter.

Ben pressed kisses on Sai's neck, little gentle ones as Sai pulled himself together. He could tell the exact moment Sai was okay: the set of his shoulders shifted, the line of his back did too. The change was subtle, but it caught Ben's attention like a flare.

When Sai turned around, his eyes were dark, lips pressed firmly together. He brought their clasped hands up and kissed the back of Ben's knuckles. Shudders ran through Ben at the simple touch of lips against his skin.

"Ben." There was a touch of hesitation in Sai's voice.

"Yes?"

Sai kept his eyes downcast, his thumb rubbing circles across Ben's hand. "I have a certain taste in the bedroom. You may have picked up on it the last time."

Ben thought back to the way Sai had ordered him around, manhandled him and pressed him into the bed, taken control and fucked him so hard Ben's whole body had been aching and sore the next day. The sex was definitely more intense than Ben's previous experiences, and he had loved it. He couldn't wait for a repeat performance.

But "a certain taste"? He wasn't entirely sure what Sai meant. "Can you be more specific?"

Sai looked up and caught Ben's gaze. The pause was long enough that Ben wondered if Sai would drop the conversation altogether.

Sai took a deep breath. "I tend to be aggressive in bed. Other partners have taken issue with it in the past. I need to know if you are okay with it."

Ben cocked his head. "You mean the whole telling me what to do thing? And holding my hands above my head?"

Sai narrowed his eyes and twisted his lips into a half smile like he was remembering what he had done to Ben last time. "Yes, and similar things."

Ben's heart rate ratcheted up at the implication of other similar things Sai might do to him in bed. "I think it's hot."

"You like it?" Sai sounded a little skeptical, like he couldn't quite believe it was true.

"Yeah, I think I do."

"You have not had a partner like me before."

A sliver of doubt wound around Ben. Was he too inexperienced for Sai? "No, I haven't. Is that a problem?"

Sai shook his head slowly, exuding an authority that had Ben's heart skittering in its rush to keep up with the demands of his body. "No, it is not a problem. But you must tell me if I push too hard. If you say stop, I stop. If you say no, I stop. Do you understand?"

Oh yes, he understood and his mind ran wild with what Sai might do to him—with what he wanted Sai to do to him. Ben nodded.

"I have to hear you say it. Do you understand?" Sai's voice was lower now, like he was keeping himself tightly controlled.

"I understand." Ben couldn't speak above a whisper, but it must have been enough.

Sai stood abruptly and held out his hand. It was an invitation to new experiences that Ben simply could not turn down. As he slipped his hand into Sai's, his skin tingled with anticipation and his gut clenched in desire.

He followed Sai to the bed and lay back as Sai pressed him down. Sai bent for a kiss, slipping his tongue into Ben's mouth like a warm knife through soft butter, and pleasure sliced through Ben's body as their tongues met. The kiss stole Ben's breath away, leaving him dizzy, lusting for more.

"Please," he whispered, pushing Sai away with his hands.

Sai narrowed his eyes at him, but after another whimpered please, Sai allowed him the freedom to flip their positions. Kneeling next to Sai was a powerful feeling. Not because the position gave him the advantage but because Sai had willingly lain down for him, giving him the reins.

It was all the more potent given the conversation they

just had. Sai said he was aggressive; he liked to control and dictate their pleasure. But here he was, lain out for Ben to do with as he pleased.

Ben's hands trembled as he reached for the buttons of Sai's shirt and undid them one by one. Underneath Sai wore a white tank top. It hugged his body, leaving nothing to the imagination, and his nipples stood out against the fabric.

Ben drank in the sight of Sai, fit and trim from regular tennis sessions and swims in the pool. He tugged up the tank top and ran his hands along Sai's skin, the warmth of Sai's body seeping into his palms. When he reached Sai's nipples, they were already little nubs, hardened with desire, and Ben wasted no time in covering one of them with his mouth while using his free hand to tease and pinch the other. The rapid rise and fall of Sai's chest underneath him gave Ben the confidence to ghost one hand down toward Sai's crotch and palm the bulge he found there.

Sai dug his fingers into Ben's hair and held his head in place while he widened his legs to give Ben greater access. With a dexterity that surprised even him, Ben tugged at Sai's belt until it came undone and somehow managed to get his hand down the front of Sai's pants to reach his prize. He wasn't disappointed. Sai was plump and growing harder with each pull of Ben's mouth on Sai's nipple and each nip of his teeth.

"Ben," Sai growled, low and rumbly, hitting Ben deep in the core of his being. "Suck my dick."

Oh yes. Please.

Ben moved to release Sai from the confines of his pants and dove down on the beautiful cock that emerged. Ben loved to suck dick and was pretty proud of his technique. He pushed himself until his nose rubbed against Sai's neatly trimmed pubic hairs and reveled in the way Sai's cock slipped down his throat. Sai must have liked that too because the growling grew louder.

Sai tugged on his hair, and Ben came up for breath. But instead of releasing so he could continue, Sai kept him where he was with a hand on Ben's head and thrust his hips up to fuck Ben's mouth. It was Ben's turn to growl as he relaxed his throat and let Sai pump his cock in and out at his leisure.

Ben lost track of time as Sai fucked his mouth, his mind blissing out to the feeling of a cock filling his throat. By the time Sai let him go and he flopped onto his back, he was lost in a haze of lust, and all he knew was his dick was so hard it hurt. He didn't notice Sai shedding the rest of his clothes or pulling out lube and a condom from the drawer underneath the bed. He barely stirred when Sai undressed him with less-than-steady hands, fingers lingering over his highly sensitized skin.

Sai lay next to him, close enough for his dick, still hard and wet from Ben's mouth, to press against Ben's hip. "I love how hairy you are," Sai breathed as he raked his fingers across Ben's chest.

The heat of a blush blossomed across Ben's ears and spread to his chest were Sai's fingernails had left their mark on him.

"Don't be embarrassed." Sai tugged at some of the hair, and pleasure shot through Ben's body, disproportionate to the smallness of the trigger. "I like it."

Sai bent over for a kiss, and all thoughts of embarrassment fled from Ben's mind, replaced by the feeling of Sai's tongue in his mouth, Sai's hand on his dick, Sai's leg thrown over his thighs. He wasn't ready to stop kissing when Sai pulled away.

"Turn over."

Ben flipped himself around, pillowing his cheek on his

forearms. Sai worked his hands down his back, seeking out all the knots and tight spots in the same way he had during the impromptu massage on the boat. By the time those magic hands made it to his ass, Ben was a pile of goo, in danger of seeping into the mattress.

"Your muscles are so tight," Sai admonished. "You need to relax more. It's not healthy to be this wound up."

Ben moaned his agreement but was in no position to point out the irony in Sai's statement. On his ass, Sai's hands rose to the next level of wizardry. He kneaded the big muscles and worked out the kinks Ben didn't even know could exist down there. When Sai finally dipped his fingers into his crease and sought out his hole, Ben didn't have the strength to arch up and meet him halfway.

He forced Ben's legs apart with a knee between his thighs, then forced them even farther with the other one. He felt Sai tracing his hole, dipping the tip of his finger inside. First just a little to tease, then a little more until Ben was hungry for it, aching for it. But just one finger wasn't enough. He wanted to be filled to the brim, to overflowing.

He whimpered, "Please, Sai. Please."

A growl came from behind him, loud and possessive, and a shiver of anticipation ran down his back as Sai dealt with the foil-wrapped condom and leaned over him. The initial breach of his body was always his favorite part, but when Sai's dick entered him while he was held immobile by one hand pressing against the middle of his back and the other holding on to his hip, it was the best feeling in the whole world.

Ben groaned and reached his hands out to brace himself for the fucking that was sure to come. Instead Sai captured his hands and brought them around his back, held in place, wrist over wrist. He had no leverage like this, nothing to push against; he could only take whatever Sai dished out.

Ben's heart raced as he thrilled at how vulnerable he was with Sai in control.

Sai fucked him slowly at first, then fast, then slow, varying his speed and depth until Ben couldn't keep up with it. He could only lie there, moaning into the bedsheets while clenching his ass, trying to keep Sai inside of him. Sai changed his angle, and the head of his cock ran right over Ben's prostate. Bursts of pleasure shot through him, every nerve ending on high alert as wave after wave of sensation followed. He was so close, his cock trapped underneath him, pinned by the strength of Sai's fucking. He just needed one stroke, just one touch, and he would explode.

"You want to come, don't you?" Sai's voice echoed in his ear.

"Yes! Please, yes!" The pleas coming from his mouth didn't sound like his voice.

"Maybe I should make you wait." Sai's words were accompanied by little nips of his ear, and Ben's head spun with the shocks that came with each bite.

"No! Please! Please, let me come. Please!"

A growl sounded in his ear, reverberating through and filling him, distracting him from the shift in Sai's position and the hand he'd snuck under his stomach and wrapped around his cock. Suddenly he was coming, lights exploding behind his eyelids, body shaking from sensation overload. His climax dragged on with Sai's face buried into the side of his neck and Sai's dick rocking repeatedly across his prostate.

Blissed out, he was barely aware of Sai reaching his own orgasm and collapsing in a heap on top of him. He hardly noticed Sai pulling out of him and rearranging them so he snuggled against Sai's side. Ben only knew peace and calm and a satisfaction that ran far deeper than skin and bones and flesh.

# 8

*T*uesday, September 19

BEN STUCK a forkful of salad in his mouth and opened up a web browser. He stared at the blinking cursor for a moment, debating whether internet stalking Sai was a bad idea. He settled his fingers on the keyboard, but before he could type anything, Mo poked his head over the top of Ben's computer monitor. Ben snatched his fingers back from the keyboard as if he'd been caught with his hand in the cookie jar.

"Hey, are you busy this afternoon?" Mo asked with a slight frown creasing his forehead.

"Uh, nope, not really. What's up?"

"Stella needs help with that new know-your-client system. Can you walk her through it? I'm so slammed right now."

"Sure, I can do that right after lunch." Ben mentally rearranged his afternoon.

"Perfect. Thanks so much, man." Mo's head disappeared when he sat back down.

Not two seconds later, several new emails popped up in his inbox, and Ben spent the next thirty minutes answering them, his salad sitting forgotten next to him. When he finished, he went back to the blank browser and its blinking cursor. He knew he shouldn't stalk, but even as he admonished himself, his fingers drifted back to the keyboard.

He typed Sai Hei Kwok in the search bar and then busied himself with the rest of the salad before he worked up the courage to look at the results. The third hit was a link to Sai's profile at his law firm.

Ben hesitated before clicking on the link, feeling like he was invading Sai's privacy. But all this was public domain, information floating out there for anyone to see. Just because he happened to stumble on it didn't make him a stalker, right?

Sure, Ben lied to himself and clicked on the link before he changed his mind again. The picture posted on the page showed Sai with a stern look in his eyes and a slight upturn of the lips—not enough to call it a smile. He looked commanding and in control, like you could trust him to sort out your problems with cool efficiency.

Ben's stomach fluttered in reaction to the photo. A part of him thrilled at the authority oozing from the simple online picture. But then he remembered what Sai tended to use that cool efficiency for. He scanned the short biography, which listed educational credits and previous work experience that lined up with Ben's understanding of Sai's history. Then he went back to the search results.

On the second page was an article about the protests at one of the Leungs' factories. Demonstrators had tried to barricade the entrance to the factory, and they hung up a giant red banner that condemned the Leungs as barbarians. Sai was quoted in the article defending his clients and praising police for having arrested those who disturbed the peace.

Ben sat back in his chair at those words. They sounded so unlike the Sai he knew.

At the bottom of the page were links to other related articles, and Ben clicked on one. It took him to another piece of reporting that was a couple of years old, also about the Leungs and their factories. In this one a reporter had posed as an employee and snuck into a factory that was manufacturing clothing. He documented the abhorrent working conditions—long shifts, no breaks, poor pay, and forced overtime. The article had accompanying pictures; they showed dingy interiors with sketchy lighting, washrooms that looked disgusting, and workstations packed so tightly they were in violation of fire codes. And the Leungs were reported to be millionaires—multimillionaires.

Ben's salad sat like a brick in his stomach.

Sai was again quoted in this article. His comments read as banal defenses of his clients. Ben doubted Sai actually believed in the innocence of his clients, but it was still painful to see those words written in black and white.

He closed out the window, pushed away from his desk, and leaned back in his chair. The words from the articles ran through his head, clashing with the image of Sai who spoke passionately about human rights and civil liberties. Ben sat there for a while, staring up at the ceiling until the mostly empty office space began refilling with those returning from lunch. He checked the time and then picked up the phone to give Stella a ring.

She picked up almost immediately, and once Ben confirmed she wasn't busy, he headed over to her desk. It didn't take long to walk her through the new system, but when they were done, Ben didn't leave immediately.

In a low voice, as if he were inquiring about contraband, he asked, "So you're Chinese, right?"

Stella laughed good-naturedly. "Yeah, but my family's from Taiwan, not Hong Kong."

"But, like, a lot of the traditions are the same, right?"

"Yeah, sure, most of them. Why?"

"So...." Ben paused, elbows braced on his knees, wondering how best to phrase his question. "Is it a thing for children, like adult children, to do what their parents say even if they don't agree?"

Stella's eyebrows rose in surprise before she frowned. "I guess it depends on the situation. I mean, filial piety is definitely a thing, if that's what you're asking. Respecting your elders is huge in Chinese culture."

"Right, filial piety, that's exactly what I'm talking about. Aren't there limitations to that?"

"Yeah, of course. If they're asking you to do something illegal, it's probably not a good idea to do what they say."

Ben sat back, Sai's dilemma weighing heavy on his mind.

"What's all this about?" Stella asked.

"It's Sai," Ben confessed. "He's in a job he hates because his dad wants him to do it. And he kind of works for terrible people because they're friends with his parents."

"Oh shit." Stella looked sympathetic, which only made Ben feel worse about the situation.

"Is that normal?" He really hoped it was, that he could explain away Sai's behavior as a cultural difference he would never understand.

Stella grimaced. "I don't know. It sounds kind of extreme. I guess it's possible that he's so traditional that he would do what his parents said with no question, but most people in our generation aren't that traditional anymore."

Well, fuck if that didn't poke a hole in his theory. If it wasn't cultural, then it was just Sai.

"Sorry, that probably wasn't the answer you were looking for, was it?" Her smile was kind but held a hint of sadness.

Ben smiled in spite of himself and shook his head. "Don't worry about it. I'll figure it out. Thanks for your help." He stood and pushed his borrowed chair back to the desk he'd stolen it from.

"You're welcome. I'm always happy to listen or answer questions about weird Chinese cultural things. You know where to find me."

Ben took the long route back to his desk and dropped into his chair with a sigh.

He liked Sai—there was no question about that. He hadn't felt this way about a guy in a long time, if ever. But then Sai wasn't like any of his ex-boyfriends. Sai was more mature and refined, but also more complicated. So much more complicated.

Ben sat up straight as the pieces clicked in his head. He liked the complication. It was Sai's intricacies and layers Ben found so enticing. Sure, the whole thing with his parents was a little fucked-up, but that was a part of who Sai was. Ben might not understand it, but that was a challenge he definitely wanted to tackle.


Monday, September 25


"Hey, Mom!" Ben made himself comfortable on his bed and propped his phone up on a pillow for a better angle.

"Hi, Ben." Maureen's face looked a little distorted on the

screen as she leaned toward the camera. "How was last week?"

"Good! It was great! How are you?"

"Things are fine around here. Your father and I have our annual health checkups this week. Full blood tests and everything."

A little sliver of worry snaked into Ben's mind. "But you guys are both healthy and all that, right?"

"Oh, sure. It's just a routine thing us old folks have to do." She smiled at her own joke. "But tell me about how life is going in Hong Kong. Have you met anyone?"

Ben rolled his eyes but couldn't keep his ears from turning pink.

"Oh, you have!" Maureen sounded unreasonably gleeful to Ben. "Tell me who you met!"

"It's noth—" He was about to dismiss it, but whatever it was he felt for Sai really couldn't be dismissed. "It's different."

Maureen drew her brows together. "What do you mean different?"

A smile tugged at Ben's lips as he thought about Sai. "He's a bit older, he's a lawyer, and he's super smart—knows everything about everything. I could just sit and listen to him talk about stuff all day."

"Stuff? What kind of stuff?"

"Literally everything." Ben chuckled as he recounted some of their phone conversations from the past week. "The economy, politics, history. We were talking about territorial waters in the South China Sea the other day."

"That's quite impressive!" Maureen returned Ben's smile. "And what's his name?"

"Sai. It's short for his full Chinese name. He's a native Hong Kong-er."

Her smile deepened. "You know, Ben, I've never quite seen you like this before."

"Like what?" Ben drew his brows together.

"So...." She paused, searching for the right word. "So joyful."

Ben burst out laughing. "Joyful?"

"Yes, joyful. Your eyes look like they're dancing, and your smile when you talk about him...." Maureen's smile took on a doting hue. "You must really like him."

"Yeah," Ben whispered. "I do." He liked Sai a little too much, if he was honest. And the thing with the Leungs felt like a boulder balanced on the edge of a cliff, just waiting for the wrong moment to come crashing down on him.

"What's wrong?"

"What?" Ben shook off the melodramatic thought. "Oh, I'll figure it out."

Maureen's frown made it clear she didn't believe him. "Are you sure?"

"Yeah, it's just...." Ben was never very good at keeping secrets from his mom. "He's so different from everyone else I've ever dated. And... there are some things I don't really understand."

"What kinds of things?"

There was no easy way to describe it, so Ben launched into the long explanation and ended with a sigh.

"Hm." Maureen made a pondering sound. "That seems like a difficult situation."

He blinked when his mom didn't give him more. "And? What should I do?"

She barked a laugh. "Oh, honey. I don't know."

"That's not helpful, Mom." Ben frowned at his computer screen.

"I'm sorry, dear. I know you really like this man, but you've only just met, haven't you? Why don't you take things slowly and see where it leads? If things don't work out in the end, then it won't really be an issue, will it?"

If things don't work out in the end... like when Ben's assignment ends and he returns to Canada. As if things weren't complicated enough. "Yeah, you're right. Thanks, Mom."

"I'm sorry, honey. I wish I had the answers you were looking for."

Ben smiled sadly and shook his head. "It's okay, Mom. Thanks anyway."

"Well, I hate to jump ship like this, but I promised Mrs. Kirkpatrick that I would take her grocery shopping today."

Ben nodded at the mention of their old neighbor. "Tell her hello and give her a hug for me."

"I will. Take care of yourself, okay, honey? I love you." Maureen waved at the camera.

Ben waved back. "I love you too."

9
———

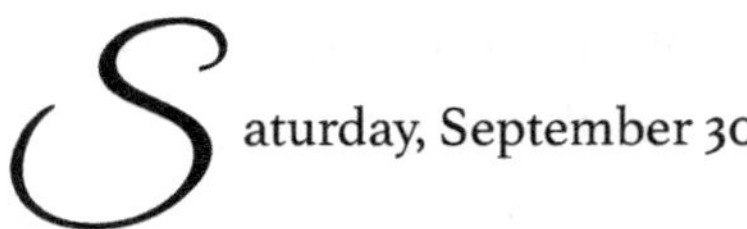

aturday, September 30

BEN THREW himself into the air and landed on the hotel bed with a flumph. Even spread-eagle, his hands were nowhere near the edges—God, he loved king-size beds. He was exhausted. He wanted a nap. No, he wanted a shower to wash off the grime of dust and sweat from walking about Macau all morning, and then he wanted a nap.

They had arrived on Friday night for the National Day holiday long weekend. They'd been late to Macau after waiting for Sai to finish some last-minute stuff at work. When they arrived, they'd gone and gorged themselves at the hotel buffet before meeting up with Winston and Jacques and a few of their other friends who had taken the ferry over from Hong Kong earlier in the evening. Ben hadn't met the others before; they were a mix of foreigners and locals, men and women, and one couple who even brought their kid.

Those without kids had ended up partying late into the

night at Club Cubic across the street from the Venetian Hotel, where they were staying. And then Sai had dragged Ben out of bed at the butt crack of dawn to go sightseeing while everyone else got to sleep in. Ben was quickly learning Sai was one of those people who needed almost no sleep— the bastard.

He supposed he should be grateful to Sai for making him go out so early in the morning. It was still cool at that hour. They walked through Senado Square, the historic center of the small city, nearly empty at that time of the morning, and they saw the remaining facade of the ruins of St. Paul's church, looming into the sky at the top of a long set of steps. They wandered the old Guia fortress that had a garden on its roof and took a stroll through the sprawling grounds of an ancient Chinese A-Ma temple.

By the time they stopped at a neighborhood called Taipa Village for lunch, the sun had been high in the sky, beating down on them with a ferocity that felt like revenge for some unnamed offense. Sai led them to a little hole-in-the-wall place for a Portuguese pork bun. It was greasy and salty, and Ben nearly died and went to heaven after the first bite. It was followed by Portuguese egg tarts, which were delicious, and Ben had seconds because he could.

All day Sai spouted off historic fact after historic fact, as if he had an encyclopedia's worth of information about Macau stored in his brain. When Ben asked how he knew everything he knew, Sai had blinked at him and said, "It's just history," like it was the most normal thing in the world. Ben had almost pulled him in for a kiss for being so cute.

"Are you alive in there?" Sai called from the living room of their suite.

"Barely." Ben made a point to sound more pitiful than he felt.

Sai wandered in, looking just as put together as he had

when they first set out in the morning. How did he manage that in the heat? The guy didn't sleep, didn't sweat. Was he even human?

Ben felt the burn of Sai's gaze wander over his body, matched with the teasing grin and dark look in his eyes. Wait—did Sai find this attractive? He was lying spread-eagle on the bed, his hair a tangled mess, his clothes askew with patches of damp where he sweated through the fabric.

"I thought you said you were going to shower." Sai stood in between Ben's feet where they hung off the edge of the bed and wrapped a hand firmly around Ben's ankle. The touch was solid, but Sai slid his thumb slowly in circles across his skin. It was at once a caress and a hold, gentle and secure. How could just one touch send Ben's insides fluttering and drive all rational thought out of his head?

"We have some time before meeting the others for dinner."

Ben almost missed Sai's rumbling words, distracted as he was by the hand on his ankle. "Huh?"

An amused smile graced Sai's lips. "What do you want to do before dinner? We could take a gondola ride...."

Ben perked at the mention of the gondolas. He'd forgotten the Venetian in Macau was essentially a replica of the Venetian in Las Vegas, complete with a canal and gondolas for hire.

Sai laughed at his reaction, slapping Ben's ankle lightly. "That's what I thought. Go take a shower, and then we can go downstairs."

He was tempted to invite Sai into the shower with him —it was definitely big enough for both of them—but Sai had already wandered back out to the living room, cell phone in hand. And then a minute later, the sounds of the TV filtered in. Ben sighed. So he'd shower alone. But damn, he'd like to get wet with Sai at some point. The thought made his dick plump as he stripped and stepped under the warm spray.

Sai popped in for a shower after Ben was done, and when he came out with his black hair slicked back and wet, Ben wanted nothing more than to run his fingers through it and drag Sai to bed. He settled for some lingering kisses, lazy and sweet, right before they headed out.

Finding a gondola wasn't difficult—they were lined up waiting for passengers, and the canal looked a little crowded with the number of slim boats drifting past each other. They settled in one, and Ben snuggled down when Sai reached his arm around the back of the seat.

"Tell me, Ben," Sai said quietly. "Why did you really want to come to Hong Kong?"

Surprised by the question, Ben glanced over to find Sai gazing out at the stores that lined the canal. "What do you mean?" They'd had this discussion before, a number of times, if Ben remembered correctly.

Sai didn't look at him when he continued. "You have a good life in Toronto. A good job. A good apartment. Many friends. I've been to Toronto before. It's a very nice city. You have a good relationship with your family, and they don't live far away. Why would you want to leave that all behind?"

Because he wanted to try something new—that was what he told everyone who asked him that question. But Sai had heard that answer before; that wasn't the answer Sai was looking for. Why did he want to try something new?

"Because that's all really boring." Ben's heart thudded in his chest as he put words to an idea that he'd only ever allowed to exist in his mind. "It's the same thing every single day. The same routine of work and home, work and home. Going drinking with friends in the evenings and then more drinking with friends on the weekends. I go visit my parents every once in a while, but other than that, it's the same thing day in and day out."

He knew he sounded like a spoiled brat, discontent with the happy, comfortable life he had the fortune of being born into.

"But you want something more." It was a statement. Not a question. As if Sai had read the yearnings of his heart.

"Yeah. I mean, I don't want to sound ungrateful. I'm really lucky to have what I have. But I've always wondered if that's all there was to life. Just...." Ben sighed. "The same old thing." He paused, his next words caught in his throat. But when Sai didn't fill the silence between them, Ben let them out into the world in a whisper. "Isn't there something more substantial than just that? More... significant?"

Their gondola driver was singing; he had a nice voice. But Ben wasn't listening to what he sung. He wasn't looking at the colorfully painted ceiling or the bright lights of the stores they drifted past. It was just him and Sai in the open privacy of their gondola ride.

It was several moments before Sai spoke. "Have you found those things in Hong Kong?"

He felt more than saw Sai gazing at him, those dark eyes watching for each change in expression. Hong Kong was fun, different, exciting. But did it make life more significant? "I don't know." Ben turned and met Sai's eyes. "It's challenging. Figuring out a new city. The culture is so different from what I'm used to. The language...." He shook his head and threw his hands in the air in defeat. "But I like it. I like that I don't feel completely comfortable here."

Sai's eyebrows shot up. "Really?"

"Yeah, that's weird, isn't it?"

Sai cocked his head, and his lips tilted into a teasing grin. "A little."

"Shut up."

Sai's grin grew to a full-blown smile and then laughter, the sound rolling through Ben in waves of satisfaction. He loved that he could make Sai laugh.

"I like it here." Ben said it again in all seriousness, gazing at Sai and realizing he didn't just mean the city.

The laughter faded from Sai's eyes and was replaced by that dark, brooding look that made Ben's insides tremble. He knew Ben wasn't just talking about the city either. One month down and two to go. Two more months to get to know Sai and fall in love. Ben wasn't there yet, but he had a feeling he could be, if they continued down this path and let the current of the waters drive them forward. The alternative was to jump off the boat, but even the thought of it made Ben feel like he would drown.

Sai blinked and looked away first.

Their gondola ride came to an end, and the boat pulled up to the steps that would take them back to the real world. Ben wanted to stay on the boat and have another go-around. But Sai had already stepped out and was reaching his hand back to help Ben off.

When he slipped his hand into Sai's, he got a reassuring little squeeze. It wasn't much, and it didn't resolve the question of what the hell they were doing with this little relationship they'd developed—but it was enough for now. Ben squeezed back.


Sunday, October 1


Winston cornered Sai after dinner as they were leaving the hotel restaurant. Amy was with him, one of their childhood friends who had brought along her husband and their son to the group vacation. They both wore stern expressions, and Sai knew he wasn't going to like whatever it was they wanted to say.

"You're in dangerous territory," Winston started.

"I agree. I didn't believe it when I first heard about it. But now that I've seen it with my own eyes, it's true," Amy chimed in.

"What are you talking about?" Sai frowned and craned his neck to peer past them to where Ben was strolling farther away with Jacques, oblivious that Sai had been detained.

"That." Winston pointed at his face, and Sai batted his hand away. Winston turned to Amy. "Did you see that?"

"Yes, I did." Amy nodded and pinned Sai with the same don't-try-to-fool-me look she used on her son.

"See what?"

"The look. It's your possessive look." Winston emphasized the word with a mocking half smile.

"What the hell is that supposed to mean?" Sai folded his arms across his chest.

"It's the look you get when you're falling for someone," Amy explained.

"What?" Sai couldn't believe he was hearing this. "I don't have a look."

"Yes, you do," Winston replied. "But that's not the point. The point is that you're falling for the guy, but he's leaving in two months. Don't break the golden rule: don't date foreigners, because they leave."

"You're dating a foreigner."

"Jacques is different." Winston waved it off. "He's not leaving. He's practically more Chinese than French."

"So maybe Ben is different too."

Two sets of eyebrows shot up, and Sai glared at them despite knowing he was going to lose the argument.

"Okay, fine. Maybe he's not different. But you're the one

who told me to go after Ben in the first place. And now that we're happy together, you've suddenly changed your mind?" Sai scowled pointedly at Winston, who had the decency to look contrite.

"I didn't think it would go this far. It was only supposed to be a quick lay," Winston muttered under his breath.

"Look, we're just worried about you. Remember what happened when you broke up with what's-his-name?" Amy said.

"Gar Wei," Winston supplied with a nod. "He was hot."

Sai rolled his eyes. "We didn't break up. He was transferred to London for work. We weren't a couple."

"And you were devastated," Amy continued.

"Devastated," Winston emphasized. "You worked for one month straight, slept at the office, showered at the gym, had your assistant go buy you new clothes so you wouldn't have to go home to change. It was disgusting." Winston wrinkled his nose as if he were remembering how gross Sai had been during that month.

"You're exaggerating. It wasn't that bad." Sai shook his head even as he lied through his teeth; it had been that bad. "So what is this? Some kind of intervention?" He bit out the words and threw his arms down to his sides. "Are you going to forbid me to see him?"

Winston and Amy shared a look, and Sai knew they had considered that possibility. That set him off. He curled his fingers into tight fists, digging his fingernails into his palms.

"Sai." Amy's voice was gentle, and she laid a hand on his arm. He resisted the urge to throw it off. "Just... be careful."

He took a breath and forced the anger inside to back down. "Fine."

They didn't believe him; it was written plainly on their faces. Hell, he didn't fully believe himself either. But despite all his attempts to keep things casual, Ben had reeled him in until there was practically no distance between them at all. Sai had no idea how he was supposed to pull back now.

"Is that all?" He knew he was being obnoxious. They were just looking out for him, and all he'd done was snap at them.

Amy and Winston exchanged another look. "Yeah," Amy said as she dropped her hand from his arm. "That's all."

"Good." He hated how angry and ungrateful that one word sounded. And yet he couldn't quite take it back as he stalked around them to go find his boyfriend.

Sai almost stumbled at the thought. Boyfriend—when did he start thinking of Ben as his boyfriend, rather than just someone he was seeing? Boyfriend had a permanence to it, a sense of commitment Sai hadn't realized he was projecting onto the relationship.

Amy and Winston were right. He knew it deep in his heart, even if he didn't like them pointing it out to him. He was in dangerous territory, except there was nowhere else he wanted to be. It felt right to be here, to be with Ben. It terrified him, scared him to the core that Ben would one day leave.

But those smiles, those wide, innocent, clear blue eyes, the earnest questions, and eagerness to experience life to the fullest. Sai was hooked on those. And then there were those times when Ben ducked his head shyly and parted his lips in desire, when he knew exactly how to respond to Sai in bed—Sai was well and truly addicted.

They spent the rest of the evening in the casino. For someone who worked in finance and was surrounded by numbers all day, Ben was terrible at blackjack. Sai tried not to smile at Ben's mock outrage every time he lost, but he failed miserably. It was hard when the outrage was always followed by twinkling eyes and a contagious laugh. Even when he was losing, Ben was all innocent exuberance, and Sai couldn't get enough of it.

The others in the group wanted to go to another club that night. But Sai wasn't feeling up to dealing with the people and the loud music, even if it meant he could get Ben dancing all over him again. But then he didn't need a club for that. From across the group, Ben sent him a questioning look, and Sai returned it with a look of his own: he adjusted the set of his shoulders, slid his hands into his pockets, and narrowed his eyes just a fraction. Ben got the message. His mouth gaped right before he sucked his bottom lip between his teeth.

Sai made excuses for himself and Ben and ignored the pointed glare Winston hurled his way. He could almost feel the daggers stabbing him in the back as they walked away. For a split second, Sai wondered whether it was better for them to go out with the rest of the group. But then they managed to get an elevator all to themselves and Ben gazed at him through those dark-blond lashes, and all thoughts of partying became irrelevant. They would have their own party that night.

**10**

———

uesday, October 3

THE PHONE rang and rang and rang. It went to voicemail, first in Cantonese and then in English. Ben had decided he liked it when Sai spoke Cantonese. Something about that deep rumbling voice muttering sounds Ben couldn't comprehend was hot as hell—except when it was in a voice-mail message.

Then a text message came through.

Sai: Sorry, I can't talk tonight. Something's come up, and I'll be at work all night.

Weird. Sai usually worked late but had always been able to spare even a couple of minutes for them to check in. Maybe it was the long weekend they spent in Macau. Sai said he usually took work home for the holidays, but they had spent Sunday by the pool, lounging in a cabana, stealing touches and kisses behind the sheer curtains, and then Monday morning in bed with Sai turning him inside out with pleasure. Ben could still feel the delicious aches in

91

his muscles from where Sai made him hold a position while he pounded his ass.

Ben: That's okay. How was your day?

No response. Not for fifteen minutes, then twenty. Thirty minutes later:

Sai: Busy. Lots of work. Sorry, can't talk.

Ben stared at his phone. They were just words on a screen, but they screamed that something was wrong.

Ben: Are you okay? Did something happen?

Sai: No, everything's fine. Sorry. Just busy. I'll talk to you tomorrow, okay?

Ben: Yeah. Sure. Good night.


Wednesday, October 4


BEN: HEY, how's your day?

Sai: It's fine. Yours?

Ben reread the three short words, knowing something was wrong with Sai but unable to say why. There was dread in the pit of his stomach, and though it had only been two days since he'd last seen Sai, the feeling was real and tangible. He told himself he was blowing things out of proportion; he told himself that he was being silly. But still the feeling wouldn't go away.

Ben: It was okay. Long, but not as long as yours :) Can you talk?

Sai: Not right now. I'll call you later.

Later never came.


Saturday, October 7

· · ·

"So where's your lawyer, lover boy?" Mo asked as he gunned down some unnamed soldier on the TV screen.

Ben punched some buttons on his controller and watched as his character threw a grenade into a bunker. "He's busy." The excuse slipped off his tongue with as much conviction as he felt about blowing up imaginary enemies in a video game—not very much.

"So that's why you came over to take advantage of my PS4?" Mo's tone was teasing, but Ben did kind of feel bad about that.

He debated whether he should voice his concerns while clearing the bunker and picking up a cache of ammo. "I think he's giving me the brush-off."

Out of the corner of his eye, he saw Mo shoot him a quick look before turning back to the game. "Oh yeah? I thought things were going well."

"I thought so too." On the screen his character got shot in the back and fell to the ground. "But we haven't really talked since getting back from Macau on Monday."

"Maybe he's really just busy. You said things were fucked-up with his job, right?"

"Yeah...." Ben's character revived on the screen and he fired some shots in the general direction of the bad guys, hoping he'd get lucky and hit one of them.

"So maybe things are just extra fucked-up this week." A notification popped onto the screen, informing them that Mo had leveled up. "I'm tired of this map. Want to switch to another one?"

Ben shrugged. "Sure." He slouched back into the couch as the next map loaded. "I sometimes wonder if he's avoiding me."

"You think he is?"

"I don't know. He does have a demanding job. Maybe I'm being too sensitive."

They played on for a couple more minutes before Mo responded. "Man, that sucks. Is he a grand gesture type of guy? Like flowers and chocolates and shit like that? Always works with the girls."

Ben let out a dry chuckle. No, Sai didn't seem like a grand gesture type of guy—at least not one with flowers and chocolates, and certainly not if they were going to show up at his office. But Mo did have a point: maybe Ben did need to do something to show Sai he was there and committed to whatever this was, for however long they had it. The question was, what the hell was he supposed to do?


Wednesday, October 11


BEN STEPPED through the sliding doors and into the blast of air-conditioning in the 7-Eleven. The weather was finally cooling as they moved toward the autumn, but it was still too hot to be comfortable for Ben. He went directly to the row of refrigerators that held the cold drinks and proceeded to load up on as many iced coffees as he could carry in his arms.

On his way to the cash register, the local Chinese newspaper caught his eye. Or rather the picture of Sai on the front page caught his eye. Sai looked like he was giving some sort of press conference, with a million microphones stuck in his face. Ben's attention automatically went to the caption beneath the photo, and then he cursed himself when the words were all in Chinese.

He grabbed a copy of the newspaper, dropping one of the bottles while he was at it. Goddamn it. Unloading his goods on the counter, he went after the stray bottle, and by the time he came back, the cashier was already ringing up his purchase.

"Can you tell me what this story is about?" he asked while pointing to the story with Sai's picture.

The cashier took the newspaper out of his hand and made to ring it up, pausing with a questioning look on her face.

"No, I don't want to buy it. Can you just tell me what the story is about?" he asked again, pointing to Sai's photo.

She spouted a bunch of words at him that he didn't understand and then went and scanned the newspaper through anyway.

"Fine. Whatever," he muttered under his breath. He paid and grabbed the bag with his bottles of iced coffee and the newspaper and rushed out into the heat.

When he got back to the office, he took the newspaper and went in search of Macey. Macey's family was originally from Hong Kong, but she had grown up in Vancouver; she could still read Chinese pretty well. He found her in the photocopier room.

"Macey! Can I ask you a favor?"

"Sure, what do you need?" She stapled presentations together as she spoke.

"Can you translate this article for me?" Ben held out the newspaper, heart in his throat.

"This one?" She frowned in concentration as she pointed to the front-page article.

"Yeah, that's Sai in the picture."

Her eyebrows shot up. "Oh yeah! Damn, he looks hot in a suit." She winked at Ben teasingly.

He smiled because it was true, but he also really needed to know what the goddamn article was about. "Yeah, he does. Sorry, but the article?"

She wiggled her eyebrows at him before turning her

attention back to the newspaper. Ben didn't know whether she was slow at reading Chinese or whether he was just really impatient, but it seemed to take her forever. The longer she read, the deeper her frown became, and the more worried Ben got. When she finally looked up, Ben was shifting from foot to foot in his anxiety.

"Um, it's kind of complicated," Macey began.

"Yeah?"

"So this couple, the Leungs." She pointed to a man and woman standing behind Sai, the same couple Ben had seen that day at dim sum. "They're, like, moguls of some sort—in manufacturing. They've been accused of corruption and stuff, illegal lobbying of the local government and a whole bunch of things. Anyway, I think the main point of the story is that there was a huge fire in one of their factories, and several of the factory workers died. They're being sued by, like, almost everyone, it sounds like."

Damn—so this was what Sai had been dealing with. "When did the fire happen?"

"Um...." Macey scanned the page again. "A week ago? I think? And this picture was taken yesterday at the courthouse."

Ben let out the breath he hadn't realized he'd been hold-ing. Oh, Sai. He could just imagine how much stress Sai was under with a situation like this.

"Okay, thanks." Ben took the newspaper back.

"Is everything okay?" she asked.

He took a moment before answering. "I don't know. I hope so, but I'm not sure."

Ben texted Sai as soon as he got back to his desk, mentioning the newspaper article. He felt terrible about assuming the worst of Sai, thinking that Sai had been avoiding him or giving him the brush-off. Instead, it looked like things with the Leungs had all gone to hell and Sai was dealing with it alone while Ben sat at home whining about not seeing his boyfriend.

He didn't really expect a response to his text; he didn't get one. Later in the afternoon, he tried calling, and it went to voicemail. Finally he looked up the phone number for Sai's law firm online and tried that instead.

The woman on the other end of the line answered the phone in Cantonese, and when Ben asked for Sai in English, she didn't seem to understand him.

"Sai Hei K—" The line switched abruptly to classical music as Ben tried to remember how to say Sai's name in Chinese. "What the he—"

"Hello?" A different woman answered the phone this time.

"Hi, yes. I'm looking for Sai Hei Kwok, please."

"I'm sorry, sir, but Mr. Kwok is unavailable." The woman spoke with the proper enunciation of a well-educated local Hong Kong-er.

Ben sighed. "Okay, fine. But is he in the office? Can I stop by to see him?"

"Again, my apologies, but I am not at liberty to disclose Mr. Kwok's schedule, and I'm afraid he's not available for an appointment until next week." The rebuff was cool but professional.

Except Ben couldn't wait until next week. "Look, can you just tell me if he's working late again tonight?"

A polite chuckle came over the line. "Sir, I'm sorry, but I can't say."

"Okay, fine. Thanks anyway." Ben hung up and dropped his phone onto his desk a little too hard.

He turned to the internet again. It was hard trying to find information in English when the issue was so local in nature, but with some creative searching and lots of translating software, he managed to figure out that the Leungs were due in court again tomorrow. That meant Sai was definitely working late that night—perfect.

THERE WAS some kind of commotion outside, and loud voices floated through his office door, but Sai ignored them to focus on his preparation for the court appearance tomorrow. Their case was thin, almost nonexistent—the fire had broken out because the factory was not up to fire codes. When he confronted the Leungs about it after the incident, they were tight-lipped, which could only mean one thing: they had somehow paid off the fire department to approve their inspection, even though the building was a hazard. Sai felt sick after that conversation. Lives were lost, and he was involved all because of some irrational need to appease his parents.

A knock sounded at his door, and Sammie, his assistant, stuck her head in. "I'm so sorry, Mr. Kwok, but there's someone here who's insisting to see you. I already told him that you had asked not to be disturbed."

"Sai? It's me. Can you let me in? I just want to talk." Ben's voice carried through the crack in the door, and Sai dropped the pen he was holding.

What was Ben doing here? His heart fluttered at the prospect of seeing Ben again after more than a week apart. But then it sank when he realized he'd been using work as an excuse. Because as much as he wanted to dismiss Winston and Amy's intervention, their words had stuck with him. The past week had been one of the worst in his life, not just because the case with the Leungs was blowing up in his face, but also because he didn't have Ben to lean on for support. How had Ben become such an important part of his life so quickly?

"Let him in."

Sammie looked like she wanted to object, but instead she gave him a curt nod and withdrew. The door swung open as Ben entered, larger than life, all sunshine and blue skies, with a huge smile on his face. Sai couldn't help but smile back.

Seeing Ben in his office left Sai momentarily speechless. The door clicked shut behind Ben, and he glanced around before setting some bags on the coffee table in front of Sai's desk. Ben turned to face him, and the little hey he uttered seemed to pull all the stress of the past week out of Sai's limbs. He slouched back into his plush upholstered office chair.

"Hi."

Ben came around his desk, head ducked slightly, those baby blues peeking out beneath long blond lashes, and Sai felt like his heart would explode out of his chest. He pushed his chair back to give Ben room as he leaned against his desk.

"Sorry to just show up like this," Ben said. "I brought food." He nodded to the bags on the coffee table.

Sai shook his head, dismissing the apology. He was glad Ben was there, more so than he thought he would be. And that just proved Winston and Amy were right: he was in dangerous territory. No, he was way past dangerous territory. He was already off the deep end. Being in the same room with Ben did more for his frayed nerves than the scant hours of sleep he'd gotten on his office couch or the endless cups of coffee he'd consumed.

Sai reached for Ben's hand on the edge of his desk and brought it to his lips. Touching Ben, even something so simple, brought new life to his tired body. He pulled Ben into his lap. It was a little awkward—Ben was a bit too big to fit. But they made it work with Ben curling around him and

Sai wrapping his arms around this man who had somehow worked his way into his heart so quickly.

"What are you doing here?" Sai whispered against Ben's temple.

"I heard about what happened with the Leungs' factory. I saw your picture in the newspaper."

Sai responded with a kiss on top of Ben's head. Nothing else needed to be said; everything could wait until later. They just sat there, holding each other, soaking in each other's presence and refilling the wells that had gone dry. Sai's fingers found their way to the nape of Ben's neck, twirling at the soft hairs that had grown too long. He needed a haircut.

"Thank you." Sai finally broke the silence. Thank you for coming, for bringing dinner, for understanding, for being who you are.

He could feel Ben smiling where his face was pressed against Sai's neck. "You're welcome."

Sai gave Ben's hip a quick slap. "What did you bring me?"

Ben slowly unfolded himself from Sai's lap, and as he stood, Sai resisted the urge to pull him back down. Instead he caught Ben's hand and followed him to the coffee table.

"Just rice and barbecue meats. I wasn't sure what you wanted, so I got a bit of everything." He pulled the paper boxes out of the bags and opened them on the table.

"Where did you go to get the food?"

"Yung Kee," Ben said, citing one of the more famous restaurants in the city.

"And you got the roast goose?" Sai raised an expectant eyebrow.

Ben held up the box in his hand, showcasing half of a neatly chopped roast goose, glistening in its own fat and juicy sauce.

"Good boy." The words slipped out before Sai really put any thought into them.

Ben's eyes grew wide, and Sai silently cursed himself for his unconscious comment. But then Ben dropped his gaze, his ears turned pink, and a shy little smile graced his lips, stealing Sai's breath away.

He moved around the coffee table and sat on the couch. Ben settled in on the floor by his feet and leaned against his knee. He brushed his fingers through Ben's hair, combing it back as Ben made cute little whimpering sounds.

It was too much. He tightened his fingers in Ben's hair and pulled his head back before leaning down for a kiss. Their lips touched, and it felt like coming home. Ben strained up toward him, and Sai slipped his tongue inside Ben's mouth, savoring the moans Ben gave him. His stomach gurgled with hunger and he ended their kiss with great reluctance, but he liked the dazed look in Ben's eyes and the way Ben's lips swelled to a rosy red.

"Food," Sai managed to get out, albeit gravelly with desire.

Releasing Ben's hair, Sai reached for the plates and chopsticks and made a plate for Ben, piled high with barbecue meats of all sorts. Then Sai filled his own plate, and they ate in relative silence, Ben still leaning against Sai's leg. Sai hadn't realized how hungry he was until he bit into that first piece of roast goose, the flavors exploding on his tongue—smoky, salty, delicious.

After they finished, they left their plates on the table, and Ben crawled up onto the couch next to Sai. They lay down, Sai on his back, Ben draped over him. They intertwined their fingers on Sai's chest.

"You've been avoiding me." It sounded loud in the quiet room, though Ben whispered it.

Sai stilled his hand where he'd been running it up and

down along Ben's back. It would be easy to deny and blame it on work, on the crazy shit that had gone down almost the minute they stepped back onto Hong Kong soil. But that would be a lie.

"Yes."

Ben shifted onto his elbow so he looked down at Sai with a frown. "Why?"

"You're leaving soon." Acknowledging that truth made Sai's heart seize in a pain.

Ben's frown deepened. "Not that soon."

"But you're still going to leave."

"So what, you were planning on ignoring all my messages for the next month?" The hurt was so clear in Ben's voice, in his eyes, that Sai's heart seized again.

He'd been selfish, getting wrapped up in his work, worried about how he would survive once Ben went home. He hadn't stopped to think about how Ben would interpret his actions now. It was the type of thing his father would do: putting his own interests before those of the person he claimed to care about. It made Sai sick and the delicious food he'd eaten turned sour in his stomach.

He sat up. "Ben, I'm sorry." He stared at their clasped hands, fingers alternating in skin tone. By some miracle they had found each other from opposite sides of the world. But just because they fit together better than Sai had ever fit with anyone didn't mean they could ignore their differences. Sai had been remiss in not recognizing that right from the beginning.

"I have a habit—a bad habit—of working too much when something is bothering me." Sai gripped Ben's hand tightly, drawing strength from the connection to put into words truths he barely acknowledged himself. "It's easier to work. I can focus on fixing other people's problems rather than my own."

"Am I a problem?" Ben looked devastated, which was exactly the opposite of what Sai was trying to accomplish.

"No, absolutely not!" He wrapped the fingers of his free hand around the back of Ben's neck, as if to anchor them together. "If anything, you are the solution, but I have been too blind to see it. I was worried about what would happen when you went home; the fire at the factory provided a good distraction."

"You could have just talked to me about it."

Yes, he could have. He should have. The fact that that option had never occurred to him just showed how differently he and Ben were wired. Sai might have been the aggressive one in the bedroom, but Ben was proving to be the more assertive one outside of it.

"Communication is not my strong suit."

Ben cocked his head. "You're a lawyer, you talk for a living."

Sai smiled wearily. "No, lawyers argue for a living. Arguing is not typically an effective form of communication."

Ben rolled his eyes. "You can talk to me, you know. If it's about work, or your father, or even me. I want to know."

Sai's heart swelled at Ben's demand, spoken with a confidence that Sai strode for but often missed. He pulled Ben to him, cradling Ben against his chest. He couldn't guarantee that he'd always remember to talk, or that he'd know what to say. But he could try.

"Okay."

They sat in silence for a few moments before Ben spoke again. "But we still have a problem, don't we? I'm still leaving."

"Yes," Sai whispered.

"But we have now."

It was true, they did. But was now enough? Was it worth

it when Sai knew there might be heartbreak on the horizon? He squeezed Ben in his arms, probably harder than he should have. And when Ben squeezed back, Sai realized those questions were irrelevant because he was already too far gone. If now was all they had, then he would cherish every second of it.

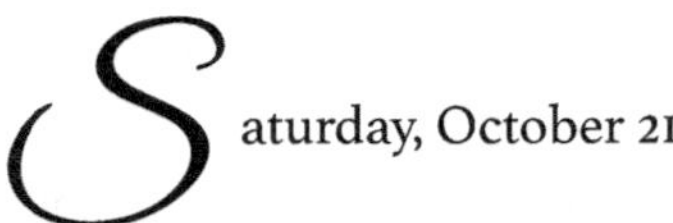

## 11

Saturday, October 21

IT WAS still dark out when Sai picked him up at his apartment. The streets were eerily silent for a city typically marked by bustle and noise. With his backpack heavy laden with supplies, Ben stumbled to a stop on the sidewalk. Parked in front of him was an honest-to-God Rolls Royce Phantom, with the back doors opening the wrong way and everything.

Sai stood between the opened door and the car, his arms resting on top of the doorframe, phone cradled in his hands. He'd been working nonstop for the past two weeks, straight through the last weekend. Ben had taken to bringing him dinner at his office, otherwise they would never have seen each other. The situation with the Leungs was still precarious but had settled enough for Ben to drag Sai out of the office for the day.

Ben had suggested a hike to get away from the city, but it was Sai who picked the trail and offered to arrange for a ride. Ben thought he had meant a taxi of some sort; never in his wildest dreams would he have imagined a Rolls Royce.

"Ben?" Sai grinned at him, and Ben could tell he was trying not to laugh. "Are you okay?"

He sputtered for a bit before his tongue managed to form words. "That's a Rolls Royce."

Sai looked at the car as if seeing it for the first time. "Oh, yeah. It's my father's. My parents are out of the country this weekend, so their driver offered to take us."

"Uh... um... your dad owns a Rolls Royce?" Ben knew Sai's family was rich, but he didn't realize they were that rich. "He employs a driver?"

Sai blinked at him. "Yes." As if that were perfectly normal.

Ben snapped his mouth shut and nodded. Okay, no big deal.

Sai stepped out from behind the door and took Ben's backpack from him. The trunk popped open, and Sai deposited it inside before holding the back door open for Ben to climb in. The interior was a rich cream color, real leather, baby soft to the touch. He stretched his legs out, and they were almost entirely straight before his feet hit the back of the front seat.

Sai slipped in the other side and called out something to the driver, who seemed so far away he might as well have been in a different vehicle. The car pulled away from the curb, so smooth it was like floating on air.

"Ben, are you okay?" Sai asked again, skepticism in his eyes.

"Yeah, this car is so cool." Ben wanted to smack himself the minute those words left his mouth. He sounded like a little kid just presented with that year's trendiest toy. Sai laughed out loud, and Ben's ears burned with a blush.

But then Sai reached over the center console and

grabbed his hand, intertwined their fingers, and brought them to his lips. He didn't say anything, but the crinkles around the edges of his eyes spoke volumes. Ben grinned back.

"There's just one thing that's wrong with this car," Ben said.

"Oh? And what is that?"

"Why is this thing here?" Ben tapped at the console separating the two back seats. When Sai frowned in confusion, Ben continued. "We can't cuddle back here with this thing in the way."

Sai burst out laughing again, this time reaching across to grasp the back of Ben's neck and pull him close for a lingering kiss. "You're right. It is an impediment." He sighed. "It appears that my parents do not place as much importance on cuddling in the back seat as you or me."

What a shame. They leaned across the barrier, shoulders touching, heads close, hands reaching. They pressed into each other all the way from Ben's apartment in Sheung Wan to the trailhead of the MacLehose Trail Section 8, deep in the New Territories, halfway to mainland China. By the time they got there, the sun was peeking over the horizon, the sky a pale, misty blue, and the air held a slight chill Ben found foreign after a month and a half in Hong Kong.

Ben grabbed their backpacks from the trunk, while Sai conferred quickly with the driver. Then it was just the two of them and the trail ahead.

"Do you need to use the toilet?" Sai pointed to the building a few yards away. "There are no toilets once we're on the trail."

Ben rolled his eyes but took Sai's advice. After they had both emptied their bladders and filled their water bottles, they were off. The trail tended upward in a relatively straight line. Trees towered on either side, letting only the strongest beams of early morning sun through the canopy.

They walked in silence, accompanied by the sound of dirt crunching under their shoes and birds chirping up above. The forest thinned a little here and there, opening to blue skies, only to grow dense again a few feet beyond. The trail grew steeper, and the stone steps that paved the way became taller. Ben's heart rate rose, and his breathing grew labored as his body adjusted to the strain of the hike.

The higher they climbed, the shorter the trees stood, and soon it was just shrubs sprouting out between large slabs of rock. Ben paused and looked around. They were at the top of some ridge, the ground falling away on both sides. In the distance stood other mountains peeking out from the fluffy white clouds. He hadn't realized how high they were already—it was breathtaking.

"Come on." Sai stood a couple of feet away. "There's more."

More? How could there be more? The hills beneath them were a variegated green from the yellowing grass to the deepest hue of the shrubs. In the distance he could see the blue of water and the gray of cities. Above were fast-drifting clouds and the bright morning sun. Ben took a couple gulps of water and continued on.

The path leveled off as they walked along the top of the ridge. It was easier on their legs, but they had lost the protection of the trees against the sun. Sweat dripped down Ben's temples and his back, but he followed Sai onward. They hiked for another thirty minutes before a simple struc-ture came into view. A steeple roof on some wooden pillars and a couple of benches underneath. They dropped their backpacks and stood in the shade to rest.

Sai pointed to the adjacent crest. "See there?" There were cylindrical buildings with white dome tops. "That's the

Hong Kong weather observatory. That's the very highest point in all of Hong Kong."

"Is that where we're going?"

"It's not open to the public. But we'll pass by it."

The highest point in Hong Kong and just the two of them with all the city laid at their feet. They were, literally, on top of the world. Ben smiled, a little light-headed at the thought.

Sai slipped his hand over Ben's, and Ben gave it a squeeze. Fingers intertwined, palm against palm—somehow it felt more intimate than when they were naked together in bed. Wandering out from the shade, they scrambled over some rocks to the edge of the mountain, where there was nothing below them but air. Hand in hand, they stood, them against the world, and Ben knew in the deepest part of his soul there was no one else he'd rather stand there with than Sai.

He stepped a little closer and propped his chin against Sai's shoulder as the clouds floated past and the wind blew on their faces. "I love it up here. It's so quiet and peaceful."

Sai didn't respond at first, and they continued to stare out at the blue sky and distant city beyond. "Sometimes I come up to the mountains like this and I don't want to go back down," he said, then paused to take several long, deep breaths. "Life is so messy and complicated, but everything is simple up in the mountains. I just walk and breathe. When I'm tired, I stop and have a drink or eat a snack. There are no demands, no deadlines to meet. It's just me and nature."

The sorrow in Sai's voice was so poignant that Ben's heart broke for him. He wanted to comfort him, but all the words that came to mind felt empty and trite. What could he possibly say that Sai didn't already know?

Sai shook his head and huffed a breath. "I'm sorry. I didn't mean to be so melancholy." He gave Ben's hand a squeeze and turned back to where they had abandoned their bags.

But Ben stood his ground and tugged him back. "Thank you for telling me. You don't ever have to be sorry for sharing things with me."

From the other side of Sai's sunglasses, Ben saw the shadow of Sai blinking his eyes rapidly. Then Sai tilted his head back as if he were gazing up at the clouds overhead. With a shuddering sigh, he dropped his head down, chin to chest.

Ben squeezed Sai's one hand and reached for the other to clasp them together. He raised them to his lips to give each one a kiss.

When Sai lifted his head again, even his sunglasses couldn't hide the raw emotion on his face. "Where did you come from, Ben Dutton?"

Ben's ears flushed at the awe he heard in Sai's voice. "Um... Canada?" He grimaced at the lameness of his own joke, but Sai burst out laughing.

It rang out loud and carefree, like the gush of water finally released from a dam. Ben smiled wide at the sound and let himself be pulled into a tight embrace. They were both hot and sweaty from the hike, but Ben molded himself to Sai anyway. Sai's breath tickled the back of his neck, and Sai's hands felt nice as he rubbed little circles around his lower back.

They stood in their embrace under the heat of the sun until Sai pushed his sunglasses atop his head and leaned back enough to look at Ben. Ben followed suit, and what he saw in Sai's eyes was everything he had ever wanted from a lover: not only love, but respect, admiration, and trust.

He leaned in and captured Sai's lips, unable to contain his hunger. He took, clinging to Sai's shoulder, searching out the corners of Sai's mouth and drawing what he needed.

Then suddenly they shifted, and Sai was kissing him, digging one hand in his hair, knocking off his hat, and angling them into a deeper embrace. Ben surrendered to it, giving Sai everything he had to give.

By the time they broke apart, panting with their foreheads still touching, everything was different. Ben couldn't quite explain it, and he didn't really want to. But an unmistakable shift had occurred, and when he pulled back far enough to look into Sai's eyes, he knew he had felt it too. The mountain had changed them.

Voices drifted up to them, reminding Ben their little paradise was far from private, and soon after, footsteps announced the arrival of other hikers. As much as he would have liked to stay on that mountaintop forever, it was time to move on.

The trail from that point forward was paved, easier to walk but nowhere near as alluring as the dirt paths of their ascent. It climbed upward, winding back and forth in switchbacks so tight Ben grew a little dizzy—he blamed it on the altitude. They passed the gated entrance of the observatory and from there started their descent.

The route down the mountain was as unromantic as their climb up was otherworldly, although the view was no less impressive. They followed the paved access road carved into the side of the mountain, their progress marked by hydro poles and cracked asphalt. Hikers taking the opposite direction crawled by them, huffing, while they seemed to fly down much faster than Ben would have liked.

All too soon they came upon a guard house and a gate that stretched across the road. On the other side was a small parking lot, and Ben spotted the Rolls Royce sitting there, waiting for them. Ben staggered to a stop, and Sai turned a couple of steps ahead.

"Ben?"

He was such a child, pouting because he had to leave a party and go home. But Sai seemed to understand his hesitation. He came back for Ben, and they stood facing each other for a couple of moments, gazing into each other's eyes and commemorating what they had just experienced together.

"Ready?" Sai breathed after a while.

Ben nodded. They were going back to the real world, but they were going back together.

## 12

riday, October 27

THE DAY after they went hiking, Sai effectively moved into Ben's little studio apartment. He had gone home after dropping Ben off and returned later that evening with a small suitcase full of clothes. Ben had already cleared space in the closet for him.

Sai still worked long days and late into the night, and Ben still brought him dinner in the evening. But then Sai would call in the wee hours of the morning to be let in, and they'd curl up together in bed, falling asleep in each other's arms.

Now it was Friday, and instead of going out with Mo and the girls, he was sitting at home, waiting for Sai to call. He had promised to leave work early. Ten thirty turned to eleven and eleven to twelve before Sai staggered in, tie swinging loose around his neck, hair disheveled and bags under his eyes so dark it looked like he'd gotten punched in the face.

"Oh my God, Sai." Ben pushed him down on the bed and started pulling off his clothes. "You look like the walking dead. You've been working too hard."

Sai let out a heavy breath but didn't argue, staring up at the ceiling, although Ben doubted he actually saw anything.

Ben kneeled on the bed and leaned over until he was in Sai's line of sight. "Seriously. You're working too hard. You have to stop."

Sai lifted a hand and threaded his fingers into Ben's hair. Even that simple movement felt tired, as if it took more strength than Sai had left in him. Ben bent lower at the small tug Sai gave him. The kiss was slow, lazy, more a way to connect than anything else.

"I need to shower," Sai muttered against Ben's lips.

"You're exhausted. You'll probably fall over in there."

"Come with me. You'll hold me up."

Ben barked a laugh. "It's too small. We won't both fit."

Sai huffed and dropped his hand back to the bed. The look of being put out was so cute that Ben couldn't resist another quick kiss.

"Let's just go to bed, and you can shower in the morning."

Sai lolled his head from side to side. "No, must shower tonight." He managed to push himself up to sitting, and Ben didn't try to stop him. He wasn't sure if it was a Sai thing or a Chinese thing, but Sai refused to crawl between the sheets without having showered first.

Dressed only in the boxer briefs Ben left him in, Sai hobbled to the washroom. A moment later the water turned on, and Ben kept an ear tuned to any unusual thumps as he gathered up Sai's clothes. When Sai emerged, he looked marginally better, and the sight of the towel wrapped low across his hips was enough to distract Ben from noticing the losing battle Sai was fighting with sleep.

Ben pulled Sai onto bed with him. "How's the case going?"

"Hm... not well. Plaintiffs are filing new suits every day."

At least that's what Ben thought Sai said. Half of it was mumbled under his breath.

"Will they combine all the suits into a class action?" Ben asked.

"No... class... act—"

And he was gone. Ben pulled the blankets up tighter and snuggled against Sai's side. It sucked that Sai worked such long hours, and he would have much preferred that they had more time together. But he was just thankful that despite it all, he still got the chance to fall asleep in the arms of the man who had stolen his heart.

Saturday, October 29

SOMETHING SHIFTED next to him, disrupting his happy peaceful place and pulling him rudely from his unconsciousness. It took Sai several moments to figure out the something was Ben, and he was trying to slip away. Sai pulled him back and tucked him more securely against his side.

"Babe, just gimme a sec," Ben muttered.

Another shift as Ben slipped through his arms, and then a slapping sound as Sai realized Ben was reaching for the side table next to the bed. It was only then the faint vibrations of a phone call registered in Sai's half-asleep brain.

"Babe, it's your phone."

No. Go away. Ben pressed the phone into his hand. He cracked one eye open, pointed it in the direction of the screen, and promptly dropped the thing onto the bed with a groan. That was the last person he wanted to talk to at God knew what hour in the morning.

He pulled Ben down and rolled over to pin Ben underneath. Mmm.... Ben made a good human pillow. If only the stupid phone would stop ringing. Even after the call went to voicemail, the phone would only stay silent for a minute before the damn thing started vibrating again.

"Babe, what if it's important?"

"It's not. It's my father," Sai mumbled, half into Ben's neck, half into the duvet caught under them when he rolled over.

"What if something's wrong?"

"Nothing's wrong," Sai insisted. "It's Chung Yeung Festival. We're supposed to go visit my grandmother's grave."

"Um, that sounds important." Ben gave Sai's shoulder a light shove. "Babe?"

Sai groaned as he rolled onto his back and grabbed the phone. "Wei?" he growled at it.

His father's angry voice came blasting through the speakers, loud enough that he had to hold the phone away from his ear. He almost didn't catch any of it, just something about it being a holiday, and he was being a disrespectful and disobedient son. The same old diatribe that usually ended with how disappointed his father was that he even had a son.

He knew Ben could hear all of it and was grateful his father lectured him in Cantonese. The weight of Ben's concerned gaze was heavy, so he kept his eyes shut tight to avoid having to acknowledge how much his father's words affected him.

"Where are you?" his father demanded, but then didn't wait for an answer. "You're at that homosexual's home, aren't you?"

Sai stiffened at the word. It wasn't derogatory, just a

scientific term to describe those who were attracted to the same sex. But the way his father said it, dripping with disgust, left no doubt as to what he thought of Sai being gay. He sat up straight in bed, now fully awake.

He wasn't even sure how his father knew about Ben. It wasn't like Sai ever told them anything about his love life. In fact, he rarely talked to them about anything if he could avoid it. It might have been the Leungs from that day at dim sum. Or someone at his law firm who noticed Ben coming around every day and decided to start some rumors. Either way, his father made sure to remind him again of how unworthy Sai was to be his son.

The ranting moved on to how Ben was distracting him from important things—namely doing whatever he could to make sure the Leungs escaped punishment for the deplorable conditions of their factories. If Sai thought his morning couldn't get any worse, he was wrong. He could count the number of times he thought he was going to be sick as he worked on the Leungs' case the past few weeks. Each time he spoke in defense of them, he felt a little bit of himself die on the inside.

"Well, we're leaving in twenty minutes. I expect you to be here." Apparently his father had concluded his ranting.

"I'll meet you at grandmother's grave." He hated how resigned he sounded, even to his own ears.

"Fine."

The line went dead, and Sai dropped the phone onto the bed. Ben's hand felt heavy on his shoulder, drawing his fingers back and forth across the hairs on the back of his neck. But Sai didn't lift his head. He couldn't meet Ben's eyes; he couldn't let Ben see what a failure he was. Too guilt-ridden to be cutthroat enough for his father, too weak to stand up for his own principles.

"Is everything okay?" Ben's voice was layered with

concern, which only made things worse. He didn't deserve Ben's concern. He was in a mess of his own making, and he had no one else to blame but himself.

Sai cleared his throat before speaking, but even then, his words came out half-broken. "I'm fine. I need to go."

Ben tightened his hand on his shoulder, and for a second he thought Ben was going to object. Part of him wanted Ben to object, to set him straight and force him to do things he wanted to do, if only he had the courage. But instead he clasped Ben's hand in his own, squeezed once, and removed it from his shoulder.

"To the office? Or to see your parents?" Ben asked as Sai climbed out of bed and headed to the bathroom.

"To my grandmother's grave with my parents, and then to the office."

A beat passed in silence, and then, "Are you going to be okay?"

With the way things were going, he wasn't so sure.


Sai pulled his Tesla over to the side of the narrow road that wound through the old cemetery built into the side of a mountain. Terraced above and below him were rows upon rows of miniature shrines to the dead. They were fashioned out of concrete and packed in so tightly that each grave site abutted the next with only inches to spare. There were thousands of them covering the east side of the mountain so the clear morning sun would shine down on the dead every day.

Other cars were parked along the side of the road, many locals following the traditions of Chung Yeung Festival to clean the graves of their loved ones. Sai spotted his parents' Rolls Royce up ahead.

He climbed the stairs that extended up as far as his eyes could see. His grandmother's grave was near the top, although technically it wasn't just for his grandmother. It was the family shrine and housed the remains of his grandfather and Sai's late uncle as well. There was room reserved for his parents when it came time for them to leave too.

His parents were already there, standing side by side, each holding three slim sticks of burning incense. Sai nodded to Ming, their driver, who stood off to the side with a bag full of supplies at his feet. Together they waited for Sai's parents to finish their prayers, bow to the grave, and insert the sticks into the waiting box of sand. In front of the box were neat little stacks of paper money and oranges arranged in little pyramids—tributes to the dead.

When his parents finally noticed his presence, the reception was cold.

"Sai Hei," his mother said. "Come pay respect to your ancestors."

His father didn't even deign to spare a glance in his direction. Sai shoved down the feeling of inadequacy that bubbled up inside. He was there to perform a ceremonial duty, which he would do as required, and then he would leave. That was all.

He took the incense Ming lit for him and positioned himself in front of the grave of his relatives. He didn't really remember his grandparents. They had both passed when he was young. His uncle passed when Sai was in middle school, and in his memory, his uncle was a lively man, easygoing and fun to be around. He never married, and Sai always wondered whether he had been gay too.

He offered up prayers, wishing his relatives a peaceful afterlife, asking to be granted wisdom, health, and happiness. Then he stuck his incense next to his parents' and stepped back.

"Sai Hei." His mother again, standing next to him,

though she didn't look at him while she spoke. "You remember Auntie Alice? She has a daughter, Joyce?"

Sai knew where this was going. "Yes, Joyce lives in California."

"Well, she's moved back to Hong Kong. She arrived last week. You should invite her to go out. You need to make new friends."

"I already have friends." This was the same conversation they had every month.

"That's why I said you need new friends." What she didn't say was she disapproved of his social circle, of Winston and Jacques and the rest. She barely tolerated those who were straight because how could they condescend to be associated with a gay man.

He didn't respond. What was there to say? He would try to defend himself, and she would huff and ignore him. Then they would rehash the same conversation next month.

His father turned to him then, acknowledging his presence for the first time since he arrived. He gave Sai a dead look, like he was the hired help and had stepped out of line. The top of Sai's head throbbed with an oncoming migraine that developed whenever he spent time in his father's presence. He needed to excuse himself before it worsened and get to the office to finish all the things he'd left pending yesterday. He needn't have worried about that.

"Don't you have work to do?" his father demanded in the same tone he used when he was upset at Ming.

"Yes, Father. I'm going to the office after we are finished here."

"You could have made it in sooner if you hadn't been at —" He was cut off by his wife's hand on his arm.

When Sai looked to his mother for an explanation, she dropped her gaze to the ground and tilted up her chin. Gratitude and sadness and frustration mixed inside of him until he didn't know whether to laugh or cry. He opted to leave instead.

"Goodbye." He nodded his farewell to his parents and then gave Ming a smile before he turned on his heel and strode back to his car. Duty done. But he didn't feel the satisfaction that supposedly came from being an obedient son. He felt dead inside.

# 13

riday, November 3

BEN STEPPED out onto the balcony of their hotel room, with the sheer white curtains rustling in the wind around him. Below was the chemical blue of a swimming pool, and beyond was the dynamic blue of the sea—all of it colored by the orange red of the setting sun. He couldn't quite believe they were there, in Thailand, in Phuket. They almost hadn't made it.

Sai had been late leaving the office, claiming he didn't want to have any loose ends dangling for their weekend away. Especially since they had both taken Monday off to spend an extra day in paradise. Ben freaked out that they would miss their flight, but Sai waved his concern away, claiming the plane wouldn't leave without them, and sure enough, they were the last two people to board.

The salty ocean breeze was damp on Ben's face, and even though it was hotter and more humid in Phuket than in Hong Kong—which Ben hadn't believed was possible—it felt freeing rather than suffocating. He closed his eyes and turned his face to the setting sun.

He smiled when Sai came up behind him and trapped him against the railing with arms on either side. Sai placed a gentle kiss behind his ear, and Ben shuddered at the intimacy of it.

"Are you happy to be done?" Ben asked.

He felt Sai scrunch his nose against his ear. "I'll never be truly done."

Ben almost rolled his eyes. "But you had the last court date for the Leungs this week. The next hearing isn't for months, right? The newspaper said it could be half a year before the next development." Sai took his attorney-client privilege seriously, and Ben had had to resort to the news to figure out when his boyfriend would have free time.

"That's true. But there is still work to be done between now and then."

Ben turned himself around and leaned back against the railing, pulling Sai in between his outstretched legs. "So then for now you're done. And you deserve a break after everything you've been through the past month."

Sai combed his fingers through Ben's hair, sending little bursts of electricity shooting through his body, but the look Sai wore was pensive and wistful.

"What is it?" He gave Sai a squeeze.

"It's nothing." Sai shook his head, and Ben squeezed him harder.

"Don't say that when it's clearly not nothing."

Sai settled his fingers at the nape of his neck, and Ben did his best to ignore them as he sought out all the knots in his muscles.

"I... I am not sure if I deserve anything."

He pulled Sai close until their hips bumped against each other, chests pressed together and Ben could bury his face into the crook of Sai's neck. The self-doubt in Sai's voice threaded through Ben like a needle lodging in his heart. How could someone as accomplished as Sai feel like he didn't deserve anything?

"Don't say that. Don't ever say that again," Ben whispered. "You deserve so much more than what those people are forcing on you."

Sai tightened his arms around him, and Ben poured all the love and admiration he felt into their embrace. Sai had to know he was better than the shoddy hand his parents had dealt him. He could do so much more with his life.

Sai threaded his fingers through Ben's hair and pulled him back to meet Sai's scrutiny. In those eyes Ben saw disbelief and skepticism but also a dash of hope. He tilted his chin up and caught Sai's lips with his own. It took Sai a moment to respond, but when he did, he was demanding and forceful, and Ben laid himself out for the taking.

Sai slipped his tongue inside his mouth and brushed it against Ben's, seeking out all the corners and stealing away Ben's breath. Sai tasted of gin and tonic and a touch of desperation, a wild scrambling for control Ben was more than willing to surrender. When they parted, Ben's head spun with desire and passion pulsed through his body.

"You look so beautiful like this," Sai whispered, eyes now dark and in command. "Lips red from my kisses, eyes unfocused, hair a mess. I could fuck you right here on the balcony."

Ben forgot to breathe. His cock twitched, and he shuddered in Sai's arms. It was so risky, so dangerous, and the thought of it sent a bolt of arousal ricocheting through him. Yes, he wanted it, and no, it was too much.

Sai's lips tilted up on one side, and he narrowed his eyes in understanding. "Hm... perhaps not today."

He stepped back, and Ben fought the crash of disappointment as Sai slipped through his arms. But then Sai clasped his hand around Ben's, and Ben followed him inside. They made it just past the open french doors before Ben found himself pressed face-first against the wall, Sai's chest flush against his back.

"How about here?" Sai whispered into his ear.

Ben's heart tripped over itself in its effort to keep beating. Yes, yes; a hundred times yes. Obscured in the shadow of the billowing curtains, Ben still felt the ocean breeze on his skin, still heard the laughter and chatter of people at the pool. He nodded, just a small movement because anything bigger and he might chicken out.

"I need to hear you say it. Is it okay here?"

Ben wasn't sure he could make his voice work. But for this, for Sai, he had to try. "Yes." The first attempt was more a croak than anything else. "Yes," he repeated.

A growl preceded another small kiss right behind his ear, and then Sai closed his teeth around Ben's earlobe and tugged. Ben bit his lip to keep from crying out, even as Sai growled at him. Sai pulled his hips back, and the hardness of Sai's dick pressed against his crack. He couldn't resist wiggling his ass against the growing bulge, and it earned him a quick smack. He gasped at the sudden pain and the accompanying spike of pleasure.

"Do you like that?" Sai asked while giving his other asscheek a sharp smack.

"Yes." Ben breathed through the rough squeeze of Sai's hand.

"Good."

Ben held on to that single word like a promise of things to come.

Sai made quick work of his pants, and when Sai wrapped his fingers around Ben's cock, Ben whimpered at the touch. Sai's body pressing into him from behind felt so good, and the sounds of water splashing in the distance made the whole thing that much more erotic. Sai knelt behind him, pushed Ben's pants down and tapped an ankle when he needed Ben to lift a foot. Then his hands were on Ben's ass, kneading the big muscles with his fingers, reminding Ben of that massage early in their acquaintance. That felt like a lifetime ago.

Ben relaxed into the massage, then tensed when Sai pulled his cheeks wide and blew a stream of hot air across his hole. Shit. Fuck. He felt Sai trace the tip of his tongue from the top of Ben's crack, down to circle his hole, then even farther to wiggle it against his perineum. Oh good God, hell. Ben was getting his ass eaten out, and just a few feet away was public space. If he cried out, he had no doubt all the people at the resort would know exactly what Sai was doing to him.

And Sai really knew what he was doing. He lapped and prodded at Ben's hole, bit his cheeks, and tugged on his balls. Ben had always had mixed feelings about rimming, especially since he hadn't taken a shower right before. But he couldn't deny how good it felt to have Sai's tongue touching the sensitive nerve endings in his most intimate of places. The dirtiness of it combined with the thrill of exhibitionism, and Ben bit hard on his bottom lip, fighting the urge to vocalize the pleasure ripping through him.

He could probably come like that, his cock throbbing with the beat of his pulse. Without thinking, he reached to give it a couple of tugs, only to have his hand slapped away. The careless gesture prompted Sai to pause the wonderful ministrations on his ass, and Ben couldn't help the small cry of protest that escaped his throat.

Sai stood up and pressed himself against Ben's back, hands firm on Ben's hips. "No touching yourself unless I tell you to. Understood?"

Ben could feel the vibration of Sai's voice across his back. He nodded.

"Say it out loud."

"Yes." Ben didn't recognize the voice that came from his throat. It was deeper than usual, throaty and laced with desire and need.

Sai growled again before he slipped his hands up Ben's sides, the pressure just slight enough to trigger the tickles, and Ben jumped with a bark of laughter. Sai didn't stop, pushed Ben's shirt up, and the tickling continued. When Ben tried to squirm away, Sai pressed him back against the wall.

Ben's cock, hard and leaking, bounced up and down in the air. He had never been aroused by tickling, but being forced to hold still and take it because it was something Sai wanted to give struck deep in Ben's gut.

When Sai finally stopped, he drew Ben's hands over his head and pinned them against the wall. "Don't move."

Ben obeyed as Sai stepped away, breathing hard, cheek flush against the wall, hands braced for balance, ass sticking out. He wondered if he looked as debauched as he felt. He couldn't see what Sai was doing, not with his face turned toward the balcony, but he could hear the rustling of clothes and the quick rip of a zipper.

Then everything fell silent. He was tempted to turn to see what Sai was up to, but Sai said not to move. So he wouldn't, not even if it killed him. Seconds ticked by, and still nothing. As Ben's heart rate decelerated to a reasonable speed and he caught his breath, he realized Sai was watching him. If he concentrated, he could hear the steady in and out of Sai's breathing and almost feel the weight of Sai's gaze on him. Ben focused all his energy on where he thought Sai stood, and an ethereal peace descended upon him, centering him, calming him.

Laughter from the pool drifted up to their suite and mingled with the feeling of Sai's tongue on his hole, the tingles of the tickles. He was still hard, and he still wanted to get off, but that was all secondary to the tranquility he felt. The dichotomy—the high of sensations and the low of serenity—pulled Ben in opposite directions until his mind spun.

It was only when Sai came back and trailed a hand down his spine that Ben was able to reconcile the two opposing forces. He didn't understand it; it didn't seem scientifically possible. But under Sai's touch, Ben found a way to be high and low at the same time, and a sob escaped him at the relief.

"You're beautiful," Sai said from behind him. "So beautiful."

A hard smack landed on his asscheek. Shock and pain radiated from the point of contact and pulled Ben toward that calming center. Then another slap. Though expected this time, the pain was no less sharp. Ben's skin tingled, his cock bobbed, and he slipped deeper into the calm. One after another, the slaps rained down across his ass until his cheeks burned and sweat trickled down his temple.

He hadn't even realized he was crying out until the slapping stopped, and Sai pressed his lips against Ben's ear. "Shh, my darling. They'll hear you."

Ben convulsed at the growled words, and then Sai pressed something against his mouth. He blinked his eyes open to see a belt, Sai's belt, folded over to double its thickness. His heart rate shot through the roof—so much for being calm. Ben opened his mouth even as his heart felt like it was going to rip a hole in his chest. Sai fed the belt in horizontally, and Ben closed his teeth over the flat broad sides. The tail and the buckle hung over his shoulder; the leather tasted salty on his tongue.

Sai pulled Ben's hips farther away from the wall, and then swung one of his feet side to side between Ben's, forcing his stance wider. Ben was going to die from a heart attack, from shame, and from the overload of sensations flooding his brain. Then Sai ran his hand along Ben's spine, wrapped his arms tightly around Ben's body, and pressed a kiss onto Ben's neck. Sai breathed slow and steady against his back, and Ben forced himself to match the rhythm. The calm stillness seeped back in until he found himself once again in that place where the dichotomies reconciled.

The initial breach of Sai's cock into his body was almost an afterthought. A formality to the way Ben already felt deeply connected to the man holding him. Even the slow shallow thrusts were a mere echo of the way Sai had already been playing him—bringing him up, then down—with little more than a word, a look, a touch. Ben let himself moan around Sai's belt, less a gag than a channel to freedom.

Sai's breath hitched in his ear, and the next thrust was a little more forceful against the tender flesh of his ass. Ben welcomed it, arching his back with a groan. That set Sai off —he snapped his hips with sharp precision, filling Ben to overflowing and then leaving him empty. Over and over again, Sai pistoned his cock in and out, and all Ben could do was brace himself, hands and elbows against the wall, and take it.

Sai gripped Ben's hip with one hand, maneuvering him so Sai could bottom out more easily. With the other hand he held Ben's head against the wall, digging his fingers into his scalp, tugging his hair. The rhythm of the fucking caused the belt buckle to jangle obscenely loud against the backdrop of skin against skin and splashes from the pool.

Sai kept him there, right on the edge of climax, inundated with sensation yet tightly reined. His pleasure was no longer his own. At some point Ben surrendered it to Sai, and it was now Sai's to bestow as he saw fit. Ben took what was given and moaned his appreciation.

"Fuck."

Sai tightened his grip almost painfully as he increased his tempo and slammed into Ben, holding nothing back.

"Fuck, Ben. I'm going to come. You're making me come."

Yes. Yes, he wanted to make Sai come. Wanted to be the source of his pleasure and release. Ben moaned again around the belt in his mouth, sinking his teeth into the leather. One last thrust, deep and soul rending, and Sai shook as Ben felt his dick pulse inside.

Then Sai pulled out, leaving Ben feeling empty, his legs quivering and his arms aching. Suddenly, Sai spun him around and pushed him against the wall. If it weren't for Sai's hand on his chest and the other on his hip, holding him up, Ben would surely have crumpled to the floor.

With the belt still between his teeth, he glanced down to where Sai knelt in front of him. His dark eyes were heavy with satiated desire, and Sai opened his mouth, only to close it around the leaking, swollen head of Ben's cock. He couldn't watch, and yet he couldn't tear his eyes away as his dick disappeared into Sai's mouth.

Hot. Wet. Sai traced patterns along the underside of Ben's length with his tongue, and Ben hit the back of Sai's throat. A couple of bobs was all he needed, along with a quick fondle and squeeze of his balls, and then he was shooting, succumbing to a force too powerful to withstand.

He did crumple to the floor then, belt falling away as he went down. Loose-limbed and empty but satisfied to the core of his being. Sai disappeared for a moment to deal with the condom and came back to join him on the floor. Ben snuggled into Sai's arms, hovering in that place between consciousness and sleep.

"I'm sorry."

Ben frowned at Sai's apology. "What for?"

"Did I push you too far?" Sai traced his fingers up and down Ben's arm, distracting to Ben's half-functioning mind. "Just now, with the wall and the belt. I'm sorry if it was too much."

Ben squeezed Sai around the chest where he was draped over him. "Don't. It wasn't too much." He buried his face into the side of Sai's neck, his next words coming out in barely a whisper. "I'd like more of that."

Sai's chest expanded in a silent gasp, and he stilled his fingers' back-and-forth motion. Then the brief tension eased from Sai's body, and Ben felt a kiss pressed into the top of his head.

"I'd like more of that too."

Ben smiled.

"Ben?"

"Mmm?"

Sai pushed him away a little and tugged lightly on his hair to get him to look up. "Ben?"

"Yeah?" He propped his chin up on Sai's shoulder.

Sai's eyes, though dark in color, held none of the darkness that stirred Ben's gut. No, they were clear of arousal and passion despite their postcoital state. Instead they were filled with so much emotion and determination that Ben sobered quickly.

"What is it?"

"Ben." Sai brushed back a stray piece of hair that fell over Ben's forehead. He kept his hand there, cradling Ben's cheek. "I love you."

Ben blinked. It wasn't that he didn't know Sai loved him. They had never said the words to each other, but Ben still knew, at some subconscious level, that Sai loved him. Just as he hoped Sai knew he loved him too. Ben hadn't thought they would actually confess those feelings to each other, not when they had one month left, and their time together was ticking down.

"I love you too." Ben put all he felt into those words, because he did. He loved Sai with everything he had—the good, the ugly, all his strengths and weaknesses.

Sai gave him a smile. It was small, but it spoke volumes: gratitude and joy, but also understanding their love was not unfettered. There were situations and circumstances standing in their way. But for now, for this moment on the floor of their hotel room, their love was enough.

**14**

*S*unday, November 5

SAI FOLLOWED Ben as they wove through the tables to the empty one at the far end of the beachfront restaurant. When the resort had advertised one of their restaurants as "on the beach," they weren't kidding. Tables were set up on the sand, and Sai was pretty sure if it had been high tide, they would have gotten their feet wet.

Still, Ben wanted to sit at the table closest to the water, and who was he to deny him? This had turned out to be a weekend in paradise—lazy mornings in bed, lounging by the pool, playing in the ocean waves—and Sai was not looking forward to going home tomorrow. Home meant a job he hated, parents who barely tolerated him, and the reality that Ben had less than a month before he went back to his home—on the other side of the world.

Not for the first time that weekend, Sai wondered if saying "I love you" was a bad idea. It seemed perfect at the time, the love welling up so strongly inside of him that he couldn't not say it. Yet it did make things more complicated for them. He tried not to think about it, telling himself to save those worries for when they left paradise, but it was difficult to turn his brain off.

After the waiter took their order, Ben reached across the table and traced a finger across the back of Sai's hand. Ben wouldn't meet his eyes, and he didn't usually play it coy.

"Ben? Is something wrong?"

Ben peeked up from under his lashes, and the tops of his ears flushed red.

Sai narrowed his eyes. "Ben?"

Ben drew his hand back, but Sai caught it and held fast.

"It's nothing."

"If it's nothing, then it won't matter if you tell me."

Ben rolled his eyes but didn't object. "I was checking my work email this afternoon."

He tugged Ben's hand. "I thought you said no work this weekend."

"Yeah, yeah, I know. Sorry." He didn't sound very sorry. "Anyway, they posted an open position onto the internal job board."

"And?" Sai prompted after Ben fell silent.

"It's for a position in Hong Kong. It's in the client relations group, and we work really closely with them. The job is outside of my expertise, but I feel like I have a good sense of what they do. I thought... maybe I should apply for it." Ben stared down at the table.

Sai breathed deep. "It's a permanent position?"

"Yeah."

Still no eye contact—that wouldn't do. He gave Ben's hand another little tug. When Ben peeked up again, he cocked an eyebrow and smiled. Ben returned the smile, and soon they were grinning at each other like idiots.

"You'd be okay with it if I applied?" Ben sounded incredulous.

"Of course I'd be okay with it. Do not be ridiculous. If you want the job, you should apply for it."

"It would mean I move to Hong Kong permanently."

Why did Ben still sound unsure? "I know. That's usually what a permanent position means."

"And you'd be okay with that? If I moved to Hong Kong permanently?"

Ben was adorable when uncertain like this. Sai pulled his hand up for a kiss on the knuckles. "I would love nothing more."

The pink on Ben's ears flushed a deeper red. "I mean, there's no guarantee that I would even get it. It's a couple of pay grades above where I am now, and I'm technically underqualified. So...." He shrugged.

"But you said you work closely with them. Do you have a good relationship with the manager in that group?" Sai asked.

"Yeah, we talk all the time when they've got new clients for us to onboard. We get along well; she seems like a good manager too."

"That's great." A thought occurred to Sai. "What about your family? Would they be okay with you moving here permanently?"

Ben shrugged. "Yeah, I mean, we've been talking over Skype, and it's been working."

Sai didn't really believe leaving his family would be as easy as Ben made it sound. "You should talk to them about it. As much as I would love having you here, this isn't a decision that you should make in haste." It pained Sai to say it, but it was true. He would never forgive himself if Ben made an impulsive decision and then regretted it.

The waiter came back with their food: rice noodles for

Sai, green curry for Ben. Their first few bites were taken in silence, and Sai wondered if he came across too harsh.

"How's the curry?" He hoped to lighten the mood.

"It's really good. Want to try some?" Ben pushed his bowl across the table.

Sai smiled. Sharing food wasn't something Ben did when they first met, but over the course of their many meals together, he seemed to have adjusted to the way Chinese people always shared their plates with each other. Sai tried a spoonful of the flavorful green curry, then pushed his plate over to let Ben try some of his noodles.

"Mmm, that's good," Ben said around a mouthful of food. "What's that called again?"

"Pad see ew. There's a good Thai place not too far from my office. We can go there next time for dinner."

Ben nodded enthusiastically, and the awkward conversation about their future seemed to fade into the background. For a moment Sai let himself imagine Ben as a permanent fixture in Hong Kong. Maybe they could find an apartment and move in together. Then they could fall asleep every night and wake up every morning wrapped in each other's arms.

It was a nice dream. And while he was at it, he could also dream about quitting his job, distancing himself from his parents, the Leungs, and that entire social circle. He could do pro bono work with legal aid. Or he could start his own firm offering discounted legal services to those most in need.

All nice thoughts. And all unrealistic fantasies that were best left to his imagination. Sai forced a smile on his face. He would take what he had right then and be content. No use longing after things that would never be.

. . .

THE IMAGE of Ben's parents loaded on his computer, both of them squeezed in close around the computer in his dad's home office.

"Hi, Ben. Can you hear us?" Maureen asked.

"Yup, loud and clear, Mom."

"Hello, son." Frank adjusted his glasses as he peered at something on his screen.

"Hey, Dad. How are you guys doing?"

"Oh, everything's fine. How was your trip to Thailand?" Maureen leaned in, pushing Frank out of the way as she spoke.

Everything's fine? Ben seriously doubted that when his mom requested this call at the last minute, but he played along.

"It was great. Thailand's a beautiful country. I'd love to go back and spend more time there. You guys would really enjoy it, I think," Ben gushed. After this past weekend, Thailand would always have a special place in his heart. He would never be able to think of the country without remembering all he and Sai had done there.

"And how is Sai?" Maureen asked eagerly. "Still busy with work?"

"Yeah, he's very busy. You remember that big case he's been working on? The factory fire?"

Maureen nodded, the image a little jumpy at the movement. "Oh, yes, that's the one with the unscrupulous owners, right?"

"Yeah, that's the one. Well, apparently something happened while we were away. The minute Sai turned his phone on after we landed in Hong Kong, the thing exploded with messages and emails from people trying to get ahold of him."

Ben remembered that moment. Sai had looked relaxed and refreshed for the first time in a long time, and as the emails rolled in, he went from happy to stressed in one second flat. Angry words had been at the tip of Ben's tongue, but he held them back and tried to be supportive instead.

"That's terrible. I hope he doesn't overwork himself," Maureen said.

Ben didn't bother to confirm his mother's fears. "Anyway, you guys wanted to talk about something?"

The mood shifted as Frank and Maureen exchanged a look. Gone were his mom's cheerful smiles and his dad's pondering expressions. A chill settled over Ben.

"What? What's wrong?" He leaned toward his computer screen, willing one of them to start talking.

Frank cleared his throat. "Well, son." He paused to pull his glasses off.

Oh shit—this looked really bad. Ben braced himself.

"I went in for my annual health exam a little while ago, and, uh, the blood work came back with something funny."

"Something funny?" Ben frowned. What was this, some kind of joke?

"Yes, well, my PSA level was above what Dr. Janick was comfortable with, so they had me undergo a biopsy."

Ben's head spun. PSA level? Biopsy? "Wait, I don't understand anything you just said. Can you start at the beginning, please?"

Frank cleared his throat again, but Maureen jumped in before he could speak. "Your father has prostate cancer, dear."

Cancer. Prostate cancer. Ben understood the words, but they didn't make any sense to him. "What?"

"The original blood tests showed elevated levels of

prostate-specific antigen. It's some sort of substance produced by the prostate, and doctors use it as a test for prostate cancer. Since your father's had an enlarged prostate for years, Dr. Janick has been monitoring his levels. They were high this time, so he had a biopsy, and they confirmed it. But they caught it early, just stage one, and Dr. Janick says it's very treatable."

Ben didn't catch everything his mom said, but he latched on to the most important part. They caught it early. It's very treatable. "When... when did you find out?"

Another shared look. Ben wasn't going to like the answer.

"Several weeks ago," Frank said.

"Several weeks? And you waited until just now to tell me?" Ben's voice rose in volume, but he didn't care. How could they keep something like that from him for weeks?

"We weren't going to tell you until you came home," Maureen shot back.

"What? Why?"

"We didn't want to worry you," she explained. "But then your father thought it might not be fair to keep it from you for so long."

"Damn right!" Then sorry when his mom raised an eyebrow at him for cursing. "Do the others know?"

They nodded in unison before Frank spoke. "Yes, that was the other reason. We wanted you to hear it from us in case any of your siblings let it slip."

"Wonderful. So I'm the last to know." Because he was on the other side of the planet. Because he wasn't there when big things were happening—important, life-threatening things.

"We're sorry." Maureen didn't sound nearly as sorry as Ben would have liked. "But we're focused on treatment right now, and Dr. Janick is very optimistic."

"So what's the treatment?"

"He likes the radiation option the best," Frank said. "I think that's what we're going to go with."

"What does that entail? And what are the other options?" Ben opened an internet browsing window, and typed in prostate cancer treatment.

"I'd have to go to the hospital every day for treatment. But he said it's noninvasive. I'd just have to lie on a bed, and they hit me with some lasers. The whole thing takes fifteen minutes or something like that," Frank explained, but Ben only half listened—he was busy bookmarking articles on prostate cancer.

"Ben. Ben!"

He switched back to the call window. "What, Mom?"

"You can do your research later. The point is that the treatment takes about three months, and he starts next Monday. Side effects should be minimal, so we're all just staying positive, okay?"

Ben sighed. What he wouldn't give to be home right then. "I should go home early. There's only a few weeks left. I'm sure they'll be okay if I leave early."

"No, don't do that—"

"There's no need—"

His parents spoke at once. "That's not why we wanted to tell you." Maureen picked up the thought. "Like you said, you only have a few weeks left. You should finish your time in Hong Kong, make the most of it while you have the chance."

"And I feel fine, son, really I do. I don't feel tired or sick or anything. There's not really anything you could do if you came back now, anyway," Frank added.

"And besides." Maureen smiled. "Don't you want to spend the rest of your time with Sai?"

Sai. Shit. He had totally forgotten about Sai—and the

conversation they had about Ben moving permanently to Hong Kong. Not that he could bring up that topic with his parents right then. He forced a smile but knew it was unconvincing.

"Yeah, okay." He couldn't have sounded less enthusiastic if he tried and then felt guilty about how unfair that was to Sai.

"We'll be fine, dear. You enjoy yourself and don't worry about us. We'll speak again before you come home, okay?"

Ben nodded at his mom's words, and then they said their goodbyes. He pushed his laptop away and crawled into bed, burying his nose in the pillow Sai used. So much for all their grand plans. It had seemed so perfect over the weekend. He would apply for the open position at work; he and Sai could find their own apartment. Maybe he could eventually convince Sai to quit his soul-draining job. Happily ever after, right around the corner. And now it was gone, dashed over the course of one internet call.

Tuesday, November 14

BEN SCANNED the crowded restaurant, and it took him a minute to spot Winston, Jacques, and the group of friends they'd all gone to Macau with. It was Amy's birthday, and apparently they had a tradition to go out for hot pot dinner every year. Ben felt privileged to have been invited this time, but as he approached the table and saw Sai hadn't yet arrived, he wondered if it had been a good idea to show up by himself. Two and a half months in a foreign country, and he still wasn't quite used to being the odd person out.

"Hi, Amy," Ben greeted the petite woman.

"Hi, Ben!" She rose from her seat to give him a hug. "Thank you so much for coming!"

"Thanks for inviting me. Happy birthday." He handed her the gift-wrapped scarf he had picked up during his lunch break.

"You shouldn't have! Thank you so much!" She took it

with a smile. "And we're delighted to have you here. You're a wonderful replacement for Sai."

She winked at him, but Ben didn't want to be a replacement for Sai. He wanted to accompany Sai. Jacques waved him over to an empty seat. There were already pots of soup boiling away on the large round table. They were called "yin-yang" pots, Sai had explained once when Ben asked about the round metal bowls with a divider down the middle, designed to keep two different flavored soups from mixing together.

"No Sai today?" Jacques asked.

Ben shrugged. "He's supposed to be here. Said he was leaving work soon when I spoke with him last."

Not that that had meant much this past week. Since returning from Thailand, Sai had been inundated with work. A news story had broken about the social circle in which the parents of many of the people around the table were a part of, including Winston's parents, the Leungs, and Sai's parents. There had long been rumors of corruption and bribery, the bending of regulatory rules, government lobbying that bordered on illegal. A group of enterprising journalists had allegedly dug up evidence to substantiate the rumors, and now Sai was in charge of damage control.

He didn't come home those first couple of nights. And when he did, he was so drained and exhausted that Ben didn't have the heart to tell him about his dad's prostate cancer. Sai had enough problems to juggle. He didn't need Ben's problems too.

Home. Funny how he thought of his apartment in Hong Kong as home—a home he shared with Sai. It was a nice sentiment, but that's all it was, really, wasn't it? A sentiment. Because Ben's real home was half a world away, and he'd be returning to it in two weeks. That was all the time they had left. Two short weeks.

He heard his name mentioned but didn't register the question that came before it, or who did the asking.

"Sorry? What was that?"

It was Amy. "I was just asking if you've had hot pot before."

"Oh, no, I haven't."

They proceeded to explain it to him. The concept was simple: they ordered plates of raw vegetables and meat, cooked it in the shared pot of boiling soup, and then dipped the food in custom-made sauces.

Under normal circumstances, Ben would be fascinated—it reminded him of Swiss fondue. But with his dad's health and the dwindling time he had left with Sai, he couldn't muster his usual enthusiasm. His dinner companions must have noticed because, after failing to engage Ben in conversation a few times, they left him alone to stew in his own thoughts.

Sai showed up halfway through dinner, sporting what was becoming his signature look: haggard with a dash of defeat. His friends gave him a hard time as he went around and greeted everyone, but when he took his seat next to Ben, all Ben got was a sad smile.

Ben returned it as his heart broke for the future they had dreamed of that was now out of their reach.

"Is everything okay?" he asked, not really sure what kind of answer he was looking for.

Sai shrugged, looking as unsure as Ben felt.

The dinner continued until Amy and her husband had to leave to relieve their nanny. The rest of them stayed behind, food devoured, just to keep chatting. Sai kept glancing at his watch, and Ben knew he had to find a moment alone before Sai slipped away again.

"Do you need to go back to the office?"

Sai had the decency to look guilty. "I should."

"I can go with you." That would give them an opportunity to talk.

Sai hesitated before finally relenting. "Are you okay with leaving now?"

"Sure." Ben nodded. They made their excuses and headed outside.

The restaurant wasn't that close to Sai's office, but Sai surprised him by suggesting they walk.

"I'm sorry I've been so busy this past week."

Ben appreciated the apology, but it only made him feel sadder. "You have a lot on your plate."

Sai lifted his head, and Ben followed his gaze up to the flashing Chinese signs that lined both sides of the street. "It's worse than what the newspapers have reported," he said so quietly that Ben almost didn't hear it.

"The corruption?"

Sai nodded. "These people are smart. They know how to cover their tracks and make sure there is no paper trail. I wouldn't have even known where to look for it."

"So then how do you know?"

A pause, and then Sai pressed his lips into a firm line and dropped his head. Maybe Ben didn't want to know the answer to his question.

"But these are your parents' friends, your parents too?" He couldn't quite wrap his mind around the fact that such corruption existed so close to him.

Sai nodded again and drew in a shaky breath. He looked so hopeless that Ben debated whether he should bring up his dad's cancer at all. But the longer he put it off, the worse it would be when he finally had to leave.

"My dad has prostate cancer."

"What?" Sai stopped short.

Ben paused a few paces ahead. "My dad has prostate cancer," he repeated.

Sai's mouth gaped, and he dropped his head down for a moment before he seemed to pull himself together. He set his shoulders into a stronger line, and he lifted his chin with an air of determination.

"I'm so sorry, Ben."

Ben nodded as they stood on the busy sidewalk, chaos all around their little bubble of silence.

"What is your father's prognosis?" Sai's voice was soft and gentle.

"They caught it early. It's treatable." That was the mantra Ben had been repeating to himself all week. "He started treatment yesterday. Says it's completely painless, so that's good."

The silence dragged on before Sai spoke again. "So I presume you will not be applying for that open position at your company."

A lump formed in Ben's throat, and pain blossomed in his chest, right where his heart stumbled over itself. "No." He could barely get the word out.

Sai nodded his agreement. "No, of course. You couldn't. You shouldn't."

A few moments later, Sai started walking again, and Ben fell into step next to him. They continued in silence for some time. After all, what was there left to say? Nothing, and everything.

So many thoughts floated around inside Ben's head. Like how much he loved Sai and how much he wished their circumstances were different. The romantic in him held out hope that they could still find some way to be together, but a trans-Pacific relationship wasn't realistic. All he could do was try to cherish the time they had left.

They paused at the intersection that would take them in opposite directions: Sai to his office and Ben back to his apartment.

"I'll see you later tonight?" Ben asked, though he didn't expect much of an answer.

"Yes, I'll be home soon," Sai replied.

Ben's heart broke at those words.

Sunday, November 19

BEN LOOKED even younger than his twenty-nine years when he was asleep, blond hair tousled, long lashes fanning across his cheeks. His bottom lip stuck out in a little pout.

At four in the morning and considering he had fallen into bed barely three hours ago, there was no rational reason for Sai to be awake—except he really wanted to watch Ben sleep. A week and a half was all they had left. He had known this was coming, saw the signs the first few times he had met Ben and all the caution signals since then. But all the warnings in the world were useless against the pull Ben had on him.

A little frown marred Ben's brow, and he twitched as if reacting to something in his dreams. "No," came the softly muttered word, and Sai hoped that it wasn't a sad dream. "Sai." Ben shifted in his sleep, swinging his arm out as if reaching for something.

Sai's heart thudded in his chest, so heavily that he was positive it would leave bruises. Ben dreamed about him. Joy and guilt clashed, and he didn't know what to feel as he pulled Ben close. Ben snuggled deep and settled back to sleep.

An errant thought had bounced around his mind ever since he learned about Ben's father. There was no way Sai could ask Ben to stay at the moment, but what if Sai went with him instead?

Canada, where he didn't know a single soul, he'd have to retake the local bar exam, and the winter was so cold that Sai shivered just thinking about it. If he really loved Ben like he said he did, could he leave everything behind and follow Ben to the other side of the world? The romantic answer would have been yes, but Sai had never considered himself a romantic.

It wasn't simply that his life was in Hong Kong, but rather Hong Kong was in his blood. Leaving his home to go to school all those years ago had been one of the hardest things he'd done in his life. He had never fully adjusted to living abroad and he had promised himself he would never do it again. What would happen to them if he went to Canada and hated it?

Sai tightened his arms around Ben, and his heart squeezed painfully when Ben nuzzled his shoulder.

He couldn't ask Ben to stay. He couldn't go with him. He had to let him go.


Sai spotted Ben in the corner booth and brought their tray of food over. He was surprised when Ben admitted he hadn't had a Hong Kong breakfast yet, and the first place Sai thought of was McDonald's.

Ben eyed the bowls of macaroni floating in soup, complete with a questionable slice of processed meat and a fried egg. "This is a Hong Kong breakfast?"

Sai laughed out loud; he couldn't help it. Ben was more than adventurous with local cuisine, and this was what he objected to?

"It's good. Trust me. When have I ever let you down?" Sai asked and then second-guessed himself. "With food."

Ben took a deep breath as if to fortify himself and then lifted a spoon of macaroni with soup to his mouth. A few quick chews and a swallow later, Ben was a convert. "It's pretty good. Definitely weird. But good."

"See? I told you."

Just as Sai picked up his own spoon to dig in, his phone vibrated loudly on the table. They both stared at the device as it bounced against the hard surface. He didn't want to answer it; he had forbidden himself to do any work today.

"You should pick it up," Ben said, and Sai loved him all the more for it.

He tapped the ignore button and slipped the thing into his pocket, where they could pretend it didn't exist.

"What if it was important?" Ben asked, head down, spoon toying with his food.

"You're important."

The startled look that melted into love in Ben's clear blue eyes when he glanced up was all the reward Sai needed for being disciplined about his phone.

Ben put his spoon down and folded his hands on top of the table. Sai got the distinct feeling he was about to get a lecture.

"Can you explain something to me? I've been trying to understand this, and I just can't wrap my mind around it."

"Sure." But Sai wasn't sure at all.

"You obviously hate your job. And I don't mean the law, because you seem to like the law well enough. But these people you work for, they're bad people." Ben raised a hand at Sai's protest. "Look, I know they're practically like family, but just because they're family doesn't mean you have to have unwavering loyalty to them.

"I mean, you've said yourself that their ethics are questionable at best and that it makes you sick to have to do some of the things they make you do. So why do you keep doing it? Just because they have no morals doesn't mean you can't have morals." Ben sat back from the table, hands thrown in the air in surrender. "Sorry. I'm sorry. It's just...." He dropped his hands with a sigh. "I wasn't going to say anything. But I can't leave without saying something."

Sai agreed with everything Ben said. It was all true. He had berated himself with those same arguments many times before, but it was the last thing Ben said that caught his attention.

"What do you mean you can't leave without saying something?"

It felt like Ben was trying to pierce him by strength of gaze alone. "You're killing yourself like this. Not just with the long work hours and no sleep. But inside it's eating away at you, isn't it?"

Ben pushed his tray of food away and leaned his elbows on the table. "Do you remember that night after Happy Valley? We were at LINQ, and you and Winston and a bunch of people were having that heated debate about civil rights and all that?"

Sai nodded—that was the night Ben's inquisitiveness first made an impression on him.

"What do you do with that person when you're at work? Because I can't imagine there's a logical way for those two perspectives to coexist inside you."

Ben was right. None of this was news to Sai, but couched in such plain language, it was impossible to dismiss just how hypocritical he had been for so long. Sai braced his elbow on the table and sank his head into his hand.

Ben wrapped his fingers around Sai's wrist and pulled his hand away from his forehead. Ben squeezed tight and didn't let go as they settled their hands across the tabletop. "I couldn't go back to Canada knowing that you're dying inside and not try to get you to quit."

Sai tried for a smile but only got halfway. "I love you." It was sappy and stupid, but he had to say it because he was pretty sure Ben was the best thing to ever happen to him.

"I love you too." Ben smiled at him. "And hey, if you won't quit for yourself, at least quit for me."

That got Sai to a full-blown smile. "You know, I was so close to it so many times these past weeks. I didn't want to keep disappointing you."

Ben cocked his head. "Why didn't you?"

Because he was a coward. He shrugged.

"You still can." Ben gave his hand a little shake when Sai didn't respond.

It was true. He still could, but it wouldn't be the same. Not if Ben wasn't around to enjoy it with him, but he nodded all the same. Ben let go of his hand and pulled the tray of food back.

Taking another bite of the macaroni, Ben scowled into the bowl. "It's not as good cold."

Sai burst out laughing. Oh dear God, he was going to be in so much trouble when Ben left.

# 16

Wednesday, November 29

THE LAST week and a half was as close to perfect as Ben could realistically hope for. Sai made an effort to leave work early, and they had late dinners together at a restaurant rather than at Sai's office. Then they went home and lazed in bed having deep discussions, or watching TV, or fucking like rabbits. They didn't step outside the entire last weekend except to meet the delivery guy downstairs when their food arrived. They marinated in each other's company, soaked each other in until Ben wasn't sure where he ended and Sai began.

Then Monday night was his farewell party. Jacques and Winston helped organize it, using Jacques's connections to book out a gorgeous rooftop patio space similar to the one where Ben and Sai had first met. Both sets of friends showed up, and Ben realized just how much he had made himself at home in Hong Kong. He was going to miss everyone so much.

At the moment, they were on the Airport Express train, scheduled to arrive at the airport in a mere twenty minutes. Sai sat next to him, their hands clutched together on the seat between their thighs. And Ben wasn't sure he was going to make it through the next couple of hours without breaking down into ugly cries.

In their last days together, he had made a point to say everything he wanted to say to Sai: that he was grateful for everything Sai had shown him and that he had enjoyed every single moment of his time in Hong Kong. He still wanted Sai to quit his fucking awful job, and most importantly, that he loved him. That he would always love him.

Now Ben had nothing left to say, but that felt like a waste. Their last moments together shouldn't be spent in silence, should they?

Ben turned at the squeeze of his hand and found Sai looking at him, eyes dark and full of emotion. Ben bit his lip to keep it from quivering; Sai narrowed his eyes and squeezed his hand harder.

Ben hesitated only a split second before he decided, fuck it, this was his last chance. He slid down in his seat and leaned his head on Sai's shoulder. Much to his delight, Sai reached his arm around the back of Ben's neck and pulled him in closer. They held each other like that, their hearts communicating all their voices couldn't say.

Ben blinked back tears when the train arrived at the airport and they headed into the terminal.

"How much time do you have left?" Sai glanced at his watch.

"Um, two hours until departure?"

Sai waved a hand dismissively. "You still have plenty of time. Come on." He grabbed Ben's carry-on luggage and turned right.

"Where are you going?"

Sai said nothing but gave him a smile that went straight to Ben's dick. There were public toilets at the very end of the terminal, and when they went inside, it was empty. Ben quickly put two and two together.

"Wait, Sai. This is a public washroom—and I have a flight to catch."

But Sai ignored all his protests and pushed him into the wheelchair accessible stall, shutting him up with a bruising kiss to the mouth. Ben couldn't help the moan that escaped him. God, he loved Sai's kisses. That tongue. Those lips. How was he supposed to live without those kisses?

The sense of urgency and their semiexhibitionist location sent all the blood in Ben's body rushing to his cock. Sai had his hands all over him, pinching his nipples, tugging his hair, squeezing his ass, and fumbling at the zip of his jeans.

He moaned again when Sai slipped his hand inside and gripped his dick with strong, skilled fingers. Then Sai pulled away and paused. Ben blinked, trying to figure out why Sai had stopped. Sai cocked an eyebrow, made the universal symbol for quiet, and sank down to his knees.

"Oh fuck." So much for being quiet.

Sai pulled down the front of Ben's jeans just enough to release his cock and balls. With a devious smile and full eye contact, Sai fed Ben's dick into his mouth. Ben bit down hard on his lip to keep from making noise, but Sai's mouth just felt too good. All wet and hot and the perfect amount of tease and pull. His hands moved of their own accord to Sai's hair, loving how the black strands felt like silk in his fingers.

Normally Sai wouldn't give him that much liberty, but very little about their situation was normal. He tightened his fingers just slightly and jerked his hips an inch. Sai's eyes fluttered shut, and vibrations from Sai's groan traveled up Ben's dick. Oh fuck. He thrust a little farther into Sai's mouth and Sai's throat constricted around him. Then

Sai palmed his balls, tugging them away from his body and giving them a light massage. His orgasm rushed forward.

Ben kept his eyes glued to where Sai's lips formed a perfect O around his dick, bruised red and glistening with spittle. He was so close; he just needed one thing. And Sai gave it to him like he was reading Ben's mind. Sai's eyes fluttered again, and he peeked up from under his lashes with a look so dark and heavy with lust that it triggered Ben's climax with nothing more than a slight twitch of an eyebrow.

Ben bit his lip so hard he tasted blood, but that was nothing compared to the rush of pleasure that tore through him. He emptied himself into Sai's mouth, spasm after spasm, and Sai drank up every last drop. He was still breathing hard and shuddering from aftershocks when Sai tucked him away and zipped him up.

Sai pushed his tongue into Ben's mouth, and Ben shuddered again at the taste of himself.

"You're bleeding," Sai accused as he pulled away.

"You said to be quiet."

"I didn't say to hurt yourself." Sai took hold of Ben's jaw and pulled it down to inspect the damage. He tsked his displeasure but said no more on the subject. One more lingering kiss, and he stepped back to run some fingers through his hair. "You have to take care of yourself."

Ben raised both eyebrows. "You have to take care of yourself."

Sai chuckled. "You're right. I do."

They left the washroom, and Ben was sure every single person knew what they had been up to. But then Sai led them over to the security line, and Ben suddenly remembered why they were at the airport. He was leaving; he checked his watch. And shit, he was going to miss his flight.

"You're not going to miss your flight." Sai really could read his mind. "You're not."

He ran nimble fingers through Ben's hair one last time and then settled them on his shoulder. Sai stepped in, mindless of the busy airport crowds, and planted a sweet, chaste kiss on Ben's lips. Ben forgave himself for the little whimper he made when Sai stepped back again.

He didn't know what to say. How was he supposed to say goodbye to the man he loved?

Sai smiled at him. "There's a saying in Chinese. 'I wish your travels to be swift and smooth, as if carried by the wind.'" He handed Ben's carry-on luggage to him.

Ben swallowed around the thick ball of emotion in his throat. "Thank you," he croaked.

"I love you." Even Sai's eyes were glistening now.

There was no way Ben was making it out of this without crying.

"I love you too." He pulled Sai back into a hug, deep and tight like he never wanted to let go. And Sai hugged him back just as fiercely.

"Now you're going to miss your flight."

Ben didn't miss the teasing in Sai's voice, but he pushed him away all the same. "Shut up."

He took his bags, and because he didn't want "shut up" to be the last thing he said to Sai in person, he murmured another "I love you" before turning to pass through security.

Ben glanced back at the last corner before he would lose sight of Sai. Sai stood there, hands in pockets, shoulders set back and straight, brows lowered over his eyes. His lips moved, and Ben recognized the three little words spoken into the air. He returned the words one last time and walked on.

. . .

"Hello?" Ben dropped his bag at the foot of the stairs and went in search of his parents. It was the weekend before Christmas, and he'd been back in Canada for three weeks. Three long weeks.

"In here!" Maureen called from the kitchen. "Have you eaten?"

It was just past eight o'clock in the evening, and Ben had driven up to his parents' home in Huntsville, about three hours north of Toronto.

"Yeah, I grabbed a bite on the way up." Ben gave his mom a kiss on the cheek and then slid onto a stool by the breakfast bar. "Where is everyone?"

"Your father and Dan are at Abigail's helping her fix something with the pipes. Joe and his brood are driving up tomorrow." His mom wiped down a spoon with a silver cloth and placed it in the small pile of glittering silverware.

Ben grabbed a knife and a second cloth and started wiping away. "How's dad?"

His dad had been undergoing daily treatment for his prostate cancer for five weeks. But the last time Ben had been up to visit a couple of weeks ago, Frank still looked fine.

"Oh, he's fine. Grumbles about having to go to the hospital every day, but he's in and out in under thirty minutes, and it's painless." Maureen waved away Ben's concern.

"Has he had any of the side effects?"

"You mean fatigue? Not really. He says he feels the same as always."

"Really?" Ben couldn't quite believe it. Whenever he heard the word cancer, he always associated it with people on their deathbeds, but his dad looked exactly as he always had for the past ten years. There were times when Ben forgot his dad even had the disease.

"Yup!" His mom smiled and dropped another spoon in the finished pile. "How are you?"

"I'm fine." He said it a little too quickly and not nearly convincing enough to fool his mother.

"Don't lie to me, young man. Tell me how you really are."

Ben put down the fork he'd been working on and twisted the cloth in his hands. "I miss him," he confessed. More than he thought it possible to miss someone. So much so that his productivity at work had nosedived, and he called in sick last Monday because he didn't want to get out of bed.

"Oh, honey." His mom reached over the counter and put her hand on his.

He bit his lip and refused to cry in front of his mother.

"Have you spoken to Sai?"

Ben nodded. "Yeah, we chat every couple of days." He sniffled and tried to blink away the tears. "It's almost harder when we talk, though. Like reopening a wound."

He felt her watching him, her sympathy overflowing in that simple gaze. It was almost too much to handle, so he slipped off the stool and went to grab the pitcher of water he knew was in the fridge.

Maureen waited until after he had downed a glass before speaking again. "I guess it would be too much to hope that he could ever move here." The silverware forgotten, she leaned against the counter, arms crossed over her chest.

Ben shook his head. "There's no way. His entire life is there. You should hear how he talks about Hong Kong, how much he loves the city, how much he wants to help change it for the better."

"But you said that his job isn't doing that—it isn't making Hong Kong better." Maureen frowned.

"I know. It's not." Ben sighed. "But if he quit his job, he could use his law expertise for so much good. If he came here, he'd have to start from scratch again. Heck, he needs a visa just to visit Canada, never mind do any kind of work."

"Have you at least discussed visiting each other?"

He shrugged. "It's come up, but we haven't made any concrete plans. I can't take time off work when I've only just gotten back."

Maureen nodded, though her brow was still folded in a frown. "You know, you should consider moving back there."

Ben stared at his mother like she had gone crazy. "What do you mean?"

"Well, you said BMO's been expanding their operations in Hong Kong. Were there any job openings when you were there?"

"Yeah, but...."

She cocked her head to the side. "But what?"

Ben still couldn't string together his argument for why he had to be in Canada.

"They're not in your area of finance?"

"No, they are."

"They don't pay well? Not the type of work you want to do?"

"No, those aren't issues."

"So what?"

"I need to be here!" Ben waved his hands around to emphasize his point.

"Here? Here where? Huntsville?" Maureen wore a grin on her face that said Ben was going to lose this argument.

"Well, no, not here. But in Toronto. With dad's health and everything, I need to be on hand."

"Oh, honey." Maureen came up to him and put a hand on his arm. "You're so sweet."

"What?" What did being sweet have anything to do with it?

"Come here." She led them to the den, and they settled on the old worn couch. "I'm going to be completely honest with you, dear. I love you; your father loves you. Your brothers and sister, we all love you. And that means we want to see you happy.

"It's sweet and endearing that you want to be close to your dad while he's undergoing his treatments, but I have to break it to you: you're not that close." She winced. "I think we spoke to you more often when you were in Hong Kong than when you lived in Toronto."

"What? That's not true." But then he thought about it. When he was in Toronto, he tried to make it back to Huntsville every couple of months, but if he was honest, it was more like once every three or four. Otherwise there might be an occasional text message sent back and forth in the interim. But in Hong Kong, he spoke with his parents every other week like clockwork. "Oh my God, it's true."

Maureen smiled at him, a little sheepish, a little apologetic. "And your father is going to be fine. Really he is. It's a slow-growing cancer, and most men with prostate cancer die of something else entirely."

"That's not necessarily comforting." Ben would rather not think about his dad dying of anything, but he knew she was right about the statistics. He had found the same information in his research.

"So what I'm saying is that if you want to be in Hong Kong, I don't want you to feel like we're holding you back.

Especially if you're going to be as miserable as you are now." She patted his knee, then gave it a quick squeeze.

His mom was telling him to go back to Hong Kong. What did he think about that? Ben blinked. He wasn't sure.

"Um, there is this one job opening in Hong Kong." He had gone to human resources to ask about it when he got back to Toronto. "They haven't had any luck filling it, and apparently my chances of getting it are good if I apply."

Maureen perked up. "Tell me more."

A smile grew on Ben's face, and he did nothing to stop it. "It's in investor relations, so not in my group, but we worked closely together all the time. I'm technically underqualified, but the manager of the other group likes me."

"Then you should apply for it." She patted him on the leg and looked at him expectantly like she wanted him to go right then.

"I don't know. I mean, it's a good job. But so is the one I have here." He winced. "I'd essentially be moving halfway around the world for a guy."

"Not just a guy. For love." She beamed as she dragged out that last word.

"Mom, my life isn't a romcom." He raised an eyebrow at her.

"I know, I know." She waved off his objection. "But still, it sounds like a great opportunity, and if that brings you back to Sai, what's wrong with that?"

"I don't even know if he'd be open to that." That wasn't entirely true. They hadn't talked about it since Ben got back to Canada, but he was pretty sure Sai would be okay with him moving back to Hong Kong—ecstatic, even. "And there's the whole visa issue. Getting a long-term work visa is a lot more complicated than the short-term one I had before."

"Oh? What does it entail?"

His ears turned red. "Um, I'm not entirely sure."

"Ben," Maureen scolded. "Why are you erecting obstacles where there are none?"

A denial was on the tip of his tongue, but damn his mom for always being right. "I don't know."

He took a shaky breath and then let it out again. He loved Sai—there was no denying that. And he loved the idea of living with Sai, seeing him every day and building a life together. But there was a huge chasm between where he was now and that imaginary future he longed for, and he didn't know how to cross it. Didn't know if he could cross it.

"I think I'm scared?" Ben dropped his chin to his chest and fiddled with the edge of his sweater. "What if it doesn't work out?"

His mom didn't have the quick and pithy answer he was looking for. She didn't seem to have any reassurances either. "That's a risk you're just going to have to take. That is if you love him enough to try."

Did he? He hoped he did, but he would never really know unless he tried, would he? Ben lifted his head and took another fortifying breath. He shared a look with his mom and then nodded.

## 17

—————

uesday, January 9

SAI STEPPED out of the terminal at Toronto's Pearson International Airport and let out the vilest string of expletives he could think of in Cantonese. He thought he'd been discreet, but a middle-aged Chinese woman glared at him out of the corner of her eye, and he quickly mumbled an apology before scurrying away.

But fucking hell, he'd forgotten how cold it was. The miserable winters he had spent in New York State were a big factor in his decision to go back to Hong Kong and stay there. He hated the cold.

Blistering wind pierced through his clothes and burrowed itself deep in his bones. He threw himself into the first available cab and gave the driver Ben's address. He just hoped to hell Ben was home.

It took about half an hour to drive from the airport into the city, and along the way, Sai stared out the window at the muted lights of the low suburban buildings and the vast expanse of inky black above. It was so different from the constant light pollution of Hong Kong that it felt like a vacuum to Sai.

As the city drew nearer, the buildings grew in height, and finally Sai saw some that might have competed with those of his home. Even then they were few and far between. The driver made a couple of turns along streets unfamiliar to Sai.

"33 Bay Street, right?" the driver asked.

"Yes, that's right."

"Should be that one there." The driver pointed across the street to a nondescript entrance, but Sai couldn't make out any address markings in the dark. "You want me to loop around?"

Sai scowled at the thought of wandering around in the dark—the cold dark. "Yes, please."

It took another few minutes for the traffic lights to change and the driver to pull the car up in front of the building. He paid and climbed out, bracing against the cold as he waited for the driver to retrieve his suitcase from the trunk. He scurried to the building the driver had indicated, and as he drew closer, the building number engraved on one of the concrete blocks became visible. Thank God he was in the right place.

Someone came out of the building just as Sai arrived at the door, and he ran the last couple of steps to slip inside before he got locked out. A reception desk sat in the middle of the lobby, but no one was there, so Sai followed the strip of carpet that led from the main entrance to the elevators.

Thirty-fourth floor.

The higher the elevator went, the faster Sai's heart beat until his hands were shaking. It must have been the jet lag from the flight or the sudden increase in altitude. But even as he stood in front of what he believed to be Ben's door and took a couple of deep, calming breaths, he knew those were all excuses.

If Ben rejected him now, he wasn't sure what he was going to do. Hell, he hadn't even booked a hotel room for the night.

He knocked. Three times. Firm, solid knocks. Then waited. And waited. He leaned in close but didn't hear any sounds coming through the door. No music, no TV, nothing. Shit.

"Sai?"

He jumped and spun around to find Ben standing behind him, black knit cap pulled low over his ears, cheeks ruddy from the cold. He looked gorgeous and Sai's heart forgot how to beat.

"Oh my God. Sai." Ben took two steps forward, then stopped. "What... what are you doing here?"

"I...." He had a whole speech prepared. He had even written it out like he did when making oral arguments in court. But standing there in front of Ben, with everything at stake, he couldn't remember a single word. "I love you," was all he could say.

Ben gasped and then let out a little sob, his hand covering his mouth. He took several deep breaths before stepping in front of Sai and unlocking the door.

"Come on in. You must be freezing. Is that all you're wearing?" Ben shut the door behind him and ushered him farther into the apartment.

"It's difficult to find coats in Hong Kong that are appropriate for Canadian winters." Sai should know; he had spent an entire week scouring the city.

"Right. Of course." Ben stripped his winter gear off, which to Sai's amusement, required a good couple of minutes. And then he took Sai's poor excuse for a winter coat and hung it up in the closet. "Do you want something warm to drink? I've got tea."

The kitchen stood right off the main entrance. Sai followed Ben and leaned against the counter as Ben pulled out a package of green tea Sai recognized from Hong Kong. Then Ben filled a couple of mugs from one of those hot water dispensers found in every Chinese home. The entire setup made Sai smile in a way he hadn't smiled in weeks.

"Come on." Ben brought the steeping tea over to the living room and set them on the coffee table.

Sai sank into the couch, the aches of trans-Pacific air travel finally making themselves known. He accepted the blanket Ben offered him because even though it was warm inside, he could still feel the winter cold in his bones.

Ben sat down close and reached for Sai's hand, rubbing it between both of his. "I can't believe you're here."

"I can hardly believe it myself." Sai chuckled.

"But... how?"

Sai couldn't help it; it was too easy. "On an airplane."

Ben rolled his eyes. "Yeah, of course, on an airplane. I meant why."

"Because...." Sai brought Ben's hand up to kiss his knuckles. The speech he had prepared came back to him in pieces. "Because I love you. And I'm miserable without you. You make me laugh, you challenge me, you take care of me when I need it, and you let me take care of you when I need that too."

Ben's mouth hung open, and his eyes were wide, glistening with unshed tears. Sai almost broke at that look, but he forged on.

"You were right about my job; you were right about everything. I don't want to be that person, I don't want to be someone you'd be disappointed in." Sai took a deep breath. "So I quit."

Ben's eyes grew wider. "You what?"

"I quit. Kind of dramatically, actually. My parents haven't spoken to me for weeks." And Sai didn't feel nearly as guilty about it as he thought he would.

"What happened? What changed?" Ben scooted closer, and their legs tangled together like they were two halves of one whole.

"I'm not sure, exactly. I got to work a little later than usual—"

"Because you were talking to me?" Ben interjected.

"Yes." Sai acquiesced the point. "I was sitting at my desk, and the phone rang. I don't know what came over me, but I picked it up and threw it across the room."

Ben gasped. "You threw your phone across the room?"

Sai laughed out loud at the horrified expression on Ben's face. "The office phone. The socket got ripped out, but the phone only suffered minor damages."

"And then what happened?"

"And then...." Sai had stared at the phone lying on the floor with complete indifference, and he realized he just didn't care anymore. He didn't care about his clients and their agendas, and he didn't care about trying to win his parents' approval. "I went to the senior partner and told him that I was quitting."

"They just let you quit?" Ben sounded incredulous.

Sai shrugged. "They don't have a choice. I turned in all my work product and left."

"Oh my God, Sai. I'm so proud of you." Ben leaned in and settled his chin on Sai's shoulder.

Sai's heart thumped in his chest at Ben's words. "I—" He cleared his throat before continuing. "I've already contacted legal aid about volunteering my legal services with them. And... I put down a deposit on a flat in the Midlevels."

He left out the part about how it was big enough for the

both of them. "I...." This was the hardest part, but he leaned into Ben and drew up all the courage he had left in his soul.

Keeping his eyes trained on their clasped hands, he ventured forward. "I know you have family obligations here. And I don't expect you to change your mind on this. But when I started thinking about what I want my life to look like, I couldn't imagine it without you."

Sai shifted and dislodged Ben's head from his shoulder. He missed the contact, but he had to say the next bit while looking at the man he loved.

A couple of tears had escaped down Ben's cheeks, and Sai brushed them away with his thumb. Then he drew his fingers through the baby-soft hairs along Ben's temples and down the back of his head to his neck.

"Ben Dutton. I love you. Would you... come back to Hong Kong with me?" It wasn't the most romantic proposition in the history of the world, but it was the best Sai could do.

He held his breath and then lost it when Ben lunged at him and crushed their lips together. Sai gasped for air, only to have Ben slip his tongue inside his mouth. Oh God, yes, he had missed Ben's kisses. How he managed to survive the past month without these kisses, Sai would never know.

"Yes, Sai Hei Kwok, yes." Ben pulled back just enough to swipe at his cheeks. "Goddamn you for making me cry."

"So does that mean...?" Sai needed to be absolutely sure.

"Yes," Ben repeated, holding their foreheads together. "Yes, I love you, and yes, I'll move back with you."

"Really?" Sai couldn't quite believe it was that easy. "But your family?"

"They're okay with it. In fact, my mom's the one who pushed me to reconsider." He sniffled, then pulled away to reach for the laptop sitting on the coffee table. "My dad's health is considered stable, and I spoke with his doctor, who reassured me that he doesn't expect any complications with the rest of his treatment."

He turned the laptop toward Sai, but Sai didn't understand what he was looking at.

"Do you remember that job opening I told you about ages ago?"

Sai nodded.

"I sent in my application last week and had my interview for it this morning."

Sai blinked as the full meaning of Ben's words sunk in. When the pieces finally clicked, pure joy exploded inside his chest. He pulled Ben in for another bruising kiss, complete with tangling tongues and tugs on hair. But it wasn't enough. Ben was his, by his choice and by Ben's own choice.

Sai pushed Ben back until they lay horizontal on the couch, the laptop set aside at just the last moment. He pressed him into the cushions, reveling in the feel of Ben beneath him. Yes, this was right; this was how they were supposed to be. Sai ran his hands along Ben's body, remembering the bumps and crevices that made Ben moan. Then he pinned Ben's hands up above his head and basked in the full-body shudders that shot through his lover.

He slipped his knee between Ben's thighs and brought it high enough to rub against the growing bulge at the juncture of Ben's legs. Ben arched up, and Sai pressed him back down, growling into Ben's mouth. He licked along Ben's jaw and nibbled at Ben's ear, then sucked on the delicate skin of Ben's neck until Ben cried out.

"Please, Sai, please."

Sai pulled back, eyes narrowed, gazing down at Ben's lust-filled dazed expression. "I love you."

Ben's breath hitched, and his lips curled into a smile. "I love you too."

# ACKNOWLEDGMENTS

My EDITOR described this story as a love letter to Hong Kong, and I couldn't have agreed more! Like Ben, I was once sent from Toronto to work in Hong Kong on a short-term assignment. During my time there, I learned to see the city as a confluence of opposites: East meets West, urban meets nature, and history meets modernity. It goes without saying that Hong Kong holds a special place in my heart!

As a Chinese Canadian, it was important for me to give an honest portrayal of Chinese culture and how it interacts with Western norms; it's complicated and nuanced and cannot be fully explored in the space of one book. But I hope I was able to highlight the challenges and beauty that result when we embrace diversity and explore both our differences and our similarities.

I want to give special thanks to my writing group for encouraging me to push on when the writing journey felt overwhelming, and especially for being insightful beta readers who nudged the book in the right direction when I didn't know where it was going.

# ABOUT THE AUTHOR

Hudson Lin was raised by conservative immigrant parents and grew up straddling two cultures with oftentimes conflicting perspectives on life. Instead of conforming to either, she has sought to find a third way that brings together the positive elements of both.

Having spent much of her life on the outside looking in, Hudson likes to write about outsiders who fight to carve out their place in society and overcome everyday challenges to find love and happily ever afters.

Hudson was a finalist and received an honorable mention in the 2017 Kayak Author Awards.

Newsletter: hudsonlin.com/newsletter/
Website: hudsonlin.com
Twitter: @hudsonlinwrites
Facebook: facebook.com/hudsonlinwrites
Instagram: @hudsonlinwrites

# ALSO BY HUDSON LIN

Stepping Out in Faith
Inside Darkness
Fly With Me

Between the Push and Pull
Embracing the Tension

Lessons for a Lifetime
Dare to Dream
Ipso Facto ILU

* 9 7 8 1 9 9 9 3 8 1 2 4 0 *